Y

D0446842

# Ignatius MacFarland:
## Frequenaut!

# Ignatius MacFarland: Frequenaut!

**by Paul Feig**

LITTLE, BROWN AND COMPANY
Books for Young Readers

Little, Brown and Company

Hachette Book Group USA
237 Park Avenue, New York, NY 10017
Visit our Web site at www.lb-kids.com

First Edition: September 2008

Library of Congress Cataloging-in-Publication Data

Feig, Paul.
  Ignatius MacFarland : Frequenaut! / by Paul Feig. — 1st ed.
    p. cm.
  Summary: Bullied in school and called "Piggy MacFartland,"
twelve-year-old Iggy longs to travel to another planet and live among
extraterrestrials, until an explosion transports him to a scary
alternate reality.
  ISBN 978-0-316-16663-8
  [1. Space and time--Fiction. 2. Science fiction.]  I. Title.
  PZ7.F333465Ig 2008
  [Fic]—dc22

                                        2007041095


                        10 9 8 7 6 5 4 3 2 1


                               RRD-C

                Printed in the United States of America

Did you know that books are supposed to be dedicated to people? I didn't, but that's probably because I haven't read that many books. I'll try to start, though, now that I'm sort of an author and everything.

So ... okay. A dedication. Um ...

I guess I'll dedicate this book to Karen and Foo. You don't know who they are yet but you will if you keep reading.

Oh, and Paul Feig, the guy who likes to think he helped me write this book, wants to dedicate it to some smart kids named Michael, Katie, and Hannah.

Whatever, Feig. My dedication was way better.

– Ignatius MacFarland
Author

## MIGHT AS WELL START
## AT THE BEGINNING . . .

My name is Ignatius MacFarland, and I am a Frequenaut.

Hmm. I guess it looks sort of weird to see it written down that way. I don't mean it's weird to see my *name* written down. I mean the word *Frequenaut*. It almost looks like it's French. It's not, though. At least not that I know of.

It's pronounced *freek-when-naught* and it's based on the word *frequency*. The naut part is the same as it is in *astronaut*, even though I don't really know what *naut* means. It's not like I'm some super smart kid or anything like that. I'm pretty average, as my report cards would be more than happy to tell you. I got so many Cs one year that my dad started calling me Ignatius C. It was supposed to be funny in a dad sort of way, but it didn't make me laugh. But that didn't stop him from saying, "Hey, there, Ignatius C!" whenever he came home from work. I knew he said it to make me realize that I should have been doing better in school, but I still wish he'd have just called me by my real name.

Ignatius MacFarland.

That's me.

I guess my name does look as weird as the word *frequenaut* when it's written down. But only to you. Not to me. Not anymore, at least.

See, I've been called Ignatius all my life. But only by my mom and dad. And my mom usually only says it when she gets mad. If I used to forget to take out the garbage or polish my dad's shoes (which was one of my main chores in the house from when I was five years old — "Can't have your dad walking around in dull-looking shoes," my mom always used to say as she handed me the stinky can of shoe polish and my dad's even stinkier shoes), my mom would yell from the other side of the house, "IGNATIUS MACFARLAND! HOW MANY TIMES DO I HAVE TO TELL YOU TO . . ." blah blah blah. Most other people call me Iggy. Iggy or Ignats. I really don't like when people call me Ignats, though, because it sounds kinda funny and people usually laugh when they hear it.

However, I'd have been more than happy to have had the kids at school call me Ignats because what they really used to call me was way worse than that. I'll tell you what they really called me if you promise never to call me it, too. I mean, now that I'm a Frequenaut and all, and since I've saved the entire human race and more and had so many adventures since the last time the kids at school saw me, there's no real reason for you to use this stupid name anyway, unless you're just trying to be mean. Seems like most of the kids in my school liked to be mean. You know, now I sorta wish I hadn't even brought this whole name thing up. But since I have, I'll just tell you what they called me and assume that you'll promise to *never* let the words come out of your mouth.

All right. Here it is. The kids at school called me . . .

Piggy MacFartland.

Pretty stupid, huh? And the stupidest part of it is that it doesn't even make sense.

First of all, I'm skinny. Too skinny, my grandma always said. She was constantly accusing my mom of not feeding me enough, but that's not true. I've always eaten lots of stuff. I just have what they call a high metabolism. It means that my body uses up tons of food because I've got a lot of nervous energy to burn it off. It's sort of like I'm one of those huge SUVs that get about ten miles to the gallon. I keep putting in the fuel and it keeps burning up before it has time to make me heavier. My dad used to say that I get bad mileage. He's a real funny guy. (And if you heard me say so, you'd know I was being a smart aleck because I'd say it like this: "He's a reeeeeeal funny guy.")

So because I'm skinny, it didn't even make sense that they called me Piggy, other than it sounds like an insult and it rhymes with Iggy. What a clever bunch of kids they were at my school. (Sarcasm again. Tons of it.)

And Mac*Fart*land is really annoying, too. It's not like I used to fart in class or anything. I don't think I'd ever farted in front of anybody at my school. Well, there was this one time in fourth grade when I was at my desk working on a spelling test and I was concentrating real hard. When I concentrate I really tense up all my muscles — my leg muscles, my arm muscles, my stomach muscles. And I guess I tightened up my stomach muscles too much because the next thing I knew, a fart came out of me. And it was a loud one, too.

Fortunately, right when it happened, Lisa Seawell did this huge sneeze right behind me. It was such an enormous, nose-emptying sneeze that she blew snot all over her test. I mean, like, a gigantic pile of it. Seriously. And everybody in the classroom started laughing. At first, I thought they were laughing because of my fart but then I turned around and saw Lisa looking down at her test with the massive green mess in the middle of it and a long string of snot running from the paper up to her nose.

When I looked over at my friend Ivan sitting next to me, he pointed at Lisa and started laughing even harder, and so I knew that my fart had gone undetected. I felt bad that Lisa had to have her terrible snot incident just so that I could be spared the embarrassment of my super loud fart, but since that big snotty sneeze was inside her anyway, it was a good thing it came out right then.

But you know what? You know what everybody at school called Lisa after that? Well, they didn't call her Snotty or Boogers or Sneezy or Ha-Choo or even Gesundheit.

They called her Lisa.

Not even Sneeza or something nose-related that *rhymes* with Lisa. They just called her Lisa. And yet they called me Piggy and there's nothing about me that even remotely looks like a pig, and they called me Mac*Fart*land even though nobody'd ever heard me fart.

That's the kind of stupid school I went to.

And it's sort of what led me to become a Frequenaut.

See, the thing is, even though I had a good home and my parents were basically really nice, I'd always felt out of place. In my house, in my school, in the world, in life in general. I know that a lot of people feel that way but I *really* felt it. It was like I was dropped on Earth by aliens or something when I was a baby but it just so happened that the aliens who left me looked exactly like human beings. So when I started growing up, nobody could tell I was an alien because I looked normal.

Well, sort of normal.

First of all, my nose is too big for my face. And so are my ears. Just like my arms are too long for my body. They practically hang down to my knees, and whenever I walk around the corner of a building or hallway, I usually hit my hand or wrist against it.

Once my grandma bought me a watch and the first day I wore it to school, I walked out of the cafeteria and smashed my wrist into the edge of the doorway. The glass popped off the front of the watch and its insides fell out onto the floor and rolled all over the place. I was so embarrassed that I just kept walking, hoping that nobody saw me. But they did. They always did. No matter how many things I did right during the day, the only time people were looking at me was when I did something stupid. And that time the person who saw me was Frank Gutenkunitz, the kid who, for some reason that I still can't figure out, hated me.

"Hey, smooth move, MacFartland. Now how you gonna know when it's time to take your retard pill?"

**Sarcasm alert:**

Frank's a reeeeeeeeeeeal funny guy.

And so that night, when I was sitting up on the roof of my garage with my telescope, which I did every night, I was looking even harder than normal for UFOs. It was my favorite thing in the world to do, even though I'd never actually seen one.

I knew a few other kids who looked for UFOs, too, like my friend Gary, but he did it because he wanted to get a picture of one so that he could become famous for being the kid who took the world's first *good* picture of a UFO. (There's tons of crappy pictures of UFOs that are all out of focus and look like paper plates that somebody threw past the camera, which is what they usually turn out to be anyway.) But that's not why I spent so much time up on my roof looking for aliens.

No, I was looking for spaceships so that I could get one to stop, pick me up, and get me outta there.

Maybe it was just because I felt like an alien anyway, or maybe it was because I thought it'd be more fun to be on another planet than to be called Piggy MacFartland every day. I just know that I figured things would have to be better in outer space, and especially on a spaceship with super smart aliens who wouldn't make fun of me.

They'd be so advanced in their intelligence that they would have changed all their mean people into nice people and would have gotten rid of things that made them unhappy and all their rulers would be good and fair and they wouldn't have to sit around and complain about politics all the time like my dad and uncle always did. I just knew that if I could get the aliens to stop and pick me up, my life would be a whole lot better.

That's what I thought back then.

## 2

## *THUNK!*

Well, that night, as I was sitting on the roof staring through my telescope, trying to find the nebula in the constellation Orion — that's the one that looks like a hunter, if you connect all the right stars in the right order and have a *really* good imagination — I suddenly heard a sizzling sound. It kind of sounded like when my mom would throw a piece of uncooked bacon into our hot frying pan. I took my eye off the telescope's lens and looked up.

Right above me was what looked like a shooting star. I'd seen a lot of them in all the time I'd been coming up on the roof, but this one was different. It was way bigger and way louder. It had a long tail and was streaming across the sky. It flew through the ladle of the Big Dipper, streaked across the

9

W-shape of the constellation Cassiopeia, and then blew past Orion's face. (I know a lot about astronomy, as if you couldn't tell.) And it wasn't just a white tail that trailed behind it. It was bluish green, with sparks flying out of it. And it looked so close that I got worried it was going drop sparks on my house and set it on fire.

I immediately swung my telescope toward the shooting star, hoping to see it close-up. I looked through the eyepiece and lined the bright object up right in the center of my lens. There it was, burning away. But it really didn't look like a shooting star. It almost looked like the back of a rocket engine.

My heart started pounding like crazy. Maybe my wish was coming true. Maybe a spaceship was coming to get me. Maybe they had read my thoughts that had gone out into the universe. Maybe as they were flying around the galaxy doing whatever it is aliens do, one of them read my mind and then looked at his friend and said, "You know, Zolton, we should stop by the Earth and pick up a kid named Ignatius MacFarland. I think he wants to come with us." (Notice how he didn't call me Piggy MacFartland? Those aliens are definitely way nicer than we are here on Earth.)

As I strained to keep the streaking light in my telescope's view, I suddenly lost sight of it. I took my eye off the lens and saw that the shooting star had disappeared behind the big weeping willow tree in our front yard. Oh, great, I thought.

What if the aliens are looking for me and now they can't see me because of that stupid tree that drips sap all over our patio? What if there's another kid up on his garage roof right now and they think I'm him? And what if he's just some dumb kid who's sitting up there with a BB gun shooting at garbage cans and cats and the aliens beam him up into their ship and call him Ignatius and the kid turns out to be some jerk who ends up shooting one of the aliens in the butt with his stupid BB gun?

Then the aliens would get all mad and beam him back down and say, "Zolton, this is a terrible planet filled with mean kids. Tell everybody in the galaxy to scratch Earth off their list of destinations. And be sure to tell them that whatever they do, they must not listen to the thoughts of some kid named Iggy because he's a bully and if you pick him up he could end up ruining the whole universe."

There was no way I could risk that happening.

So I stood and started jumping up and down and waving frantically as the streaking light reappeared from behind the willow tree.

"I'm over here!" I shouted. "It's me, Iggy MacFarland! I'm on the roof over here! Come back!"

And all of a sudden, the streaking light just disappeared into thin air. The sizzling stopped.

I picked up my telescope and looked through it toward where the light had disappeared. I scanned around for a few seconds . . . and then I saw it.

A round flying object was slowly moving toward me. It was black and silent and floated through the air like a giant Frisbee. My heart started pounding even faster. I could actually hear it pounding in my ears, feel it beating in my chest. This is it, I thought. It's finally happening. I've spent so much time waiting and dreaming of this moment and it's about to happen. I'm about to have my first encounter with an alien spaceship. I'm going to go into outer space!

It got bigger and bigger and bigger and it suddenly looked like it was going to crash into me. I lowered my telescope just in time to see —

**THUNK!**

The spaceship hit me right in my forehead. It hit me so hard that I fell backward onto the roof and my telescope flew out of my hand and rolled down the shingles, hit the rain gutter, then spun up into the air and smashed onto the driveway. I had to dig my fingernails into the roof to keep myself from falling off and smashing onto the driveway, too. I looked down toward my feet to see the spaceship. And there it was . . .

A big, plastic garbage can lid.

I heard really loud and obnoxious laughter coming from the street in front of my house. And I immediately knew whose laughter it was.

Frank Gutenkunitz's.

"Hey, Mac*Fart*land, congratulations! It came back!"

And with this, Frank and his two just-as-jerky friends, Donald Jenkins and Alex Roy, started laughing in that way that tells you they don't really think something's funny as much as they want to hear how loud they can all laugh. Well, they all laughed pretty loud.

These were the kind of guys who would make aliens stay away from Earth forever. The Earth I was hopelessly, permanently stuck on.

\*     \*     \*

That night as I lay in bed and felt the throbbing lump I now had on my forehead because of Frank and his stupid garbage can lid, I was completely depressed. For that one fantastic, amazing moment before the garbage can lid hit me I had felt better than I'd ever felt in my life. When I thought that spaceship was coming to get me, it was like Christmas morning, Thanksgiving dinner, and present-opening time on my birthday all rolled into one. It was my grandma's homemade chocolate pudding. It was the opening credits of my very favorite movie. It was everything I was hoping I would feel when I finally got the chance to leave the Earth.

And now it was gone. And for some weird reason, it didn't feel like it was ever coming back.

# THE PLANET GORPLOCK

Having to go to school the next day didn't cheer me up very much. Not that it would. I mean, don't get me wrong. I've never been a kid who hates school. But I've never been a kid who loves it, either. As far as I was concerned at the time, it was an okay place to learn stuff I didn't know, but unfortunately I had to learn all that stuff while I was surrounded by people who either didn't like me, didn't know me, or didn't *want* to know me. And except for my two friends, Gary and Ivan, who were pretty much in the same boat as I was, I didn't really feel like it was my job to get to know anybody else any more than it was their job to get to know me. What was the point, you know?

The only person other than Gary and Ivan I felt at all close to in the school was a guy who wasn't even there. No, I'm not making a joke. You see, down this one hall that leads to the library, there was a picture and a plaque on the wall honoring this guy named Chester Arthur, although everyone used to call him Mr. Arthur. Well, at least the people who still talked about him anymore called him that. To be honest, I don't think most students in the school called him anything because they never knew him in the first place. I hadn't ever met him, but for some reason I felt like I knew him. Or at least understood him.

See, he was an English teacher at our junior high about five years ago and all the teachers and kids who used to go there said that he was a really nice guy. They also said that he was sort of an unhappy guy. Apparently he was always trying to write books and plays and become famous so that he could stop being an English teacher and start being a big-shot artist guy and move to New York or California.

But nobody ever published his books or bought any of his plays or anything else he wrote or painted or composed because, well, I guess the stuff he did wasn't very good. I even heard that he made the drama club put on a musical he wrote that was so bad everybody left at intermission. But since he was such a nice guy, everybody told him the play was good and excused their having to leave by saying that the cookies the snack bar served at intermission gave them food poisoning, which didn't make him feel any better since he was also the person who baked the cookies. So he was just this cool teacher that everybody liked who was really really unhappy being who he was and probably thought that nothing he did was right.

And that's why I felt kinda close to the guy.

And it's also why a lot of people think he died.

See, the plaque under his picture read, "In memory of Chester Arthur, taken from our world by accidental means, but always and forever in our hearts." The part that says "accidental means" is where there seems to be a lot of disagreement. Because a ton of people said that his death wasn't an accident at all; they say it was something he made happen himself. Because his house . . . well . . . exploded.

The gas company blamed it on the guy who built Mr. Arthur's house and the guy who built Mr. Arthur's house blamed it on the gas company. But a lot of people in the town blamed it on Mr. Arthur. They said that he just decided he didn't want to be a teacher anymore and since he didn't seem to be good at anything else, he decided that he didn't want to be *anything* anymore. So they say one day he turned on all the gas in his house, and, you know . . .

### *BOOM!*

Nothing left of the house, nothing left of Mr. Arthur. No body, no anything.

I never knew if I believed Mr. Arthur did this or not, simply because I could never imagine *anybody* doing it, no matter how bad they felt. I mean, I've been depressed before, like after the time I tried to put on a carnival in my backyard to raise money for muscular dystrophy and nobody showed up except Gary and Ivan, but I never even thought about blowing myself up. I just ate about a thousand Oreos and went to bed.

To me, the people the people who said he killed himself just sounded like they were spreading around one of those stupid rumors that people make up when they don't have enough to think about in school, like the rumor that Mr. Calaphon, our janitor, tears the heads off of rats he finds in the boiler room and drinks their brains. I mean, Mr. Calaphon is sort of a weird guy, but there's no way he's rat-brain-drinking weird.

But whether Mr. Arthur really blew himself up on purpose or not, I still liked the guy, since even his face in the picture looked like he was sort of lost and trapped, which I could completely relate to. I guess he found a way to get out of coming to that stupid school every day. It just wasn't a way I would ever choose.

\*　　\*　　\*

As I sat in my science class and listened to Mr. Andriasco tell us about how dinosaurs had evolved into birds, I couldn't concentrate. Since Ben Kramer was sitting in the desk in front of me, and since Ben Kramer weighs about fifty more pounds than I do and Mr. Andriasco couldn't see me from

the chalkboard if Ben was sitting in front of my desk, I was doodling in my notebook instead of taking notes. I couldn't help it. When I get upset about something, I can't seem to concentrate on anything except what's bothering me. And right then, I was drawing spaceships and aliens and whole new worlds in my notebook because that's what was on my mind.

"Evolution takes a very, very, *very* long time," I heard Mr. Andriasco saying as he wrote something on the chalkboard. His voice sounded really far away and echoey to me, like when the TV's on and you're about to fall asleep. "All things on this earth evolved through the processes of elimination and mutation. If something was eliminated, its genes ended and it was gone. If something survived, it reproduced and eventually its genes would mutate. And if those new genes made it stronger . . ." Echo echo echo. There were times when Mr. Andriasco could be really interesting but today's lecture didn't sound like it was one of them.

Which is why I was so surprised by what happened next.

All of a sudden, right as I was drawing a third eye on the alien who was stretching out his hand to shake mine and saying, "Welcome to Gorplock, Iggy," my notebook flew out from under my pencil.

"Ah, Mr. MacFarland. I see the world of art is calling to you more strongly than the world of science."

I looked up to see Mr. Andriasco standing over me, holding my notebook up to his face, and looking at it. The expression on his face told me that there was a big load of teacher sarcasm headed my way.

"Perhaps your alien friends here would care to help you with your midterm exams, which you'll clearly need assistance passing since you don't seem to think you need to listen to my lecture and take notes." (Hey, I didn't say it was going to be *good* sarcasm. He was not a funny guy at all.)

Mr. Andriasco looked around at my classmates, who all chuckled. I'm sure not one of them found what he said to be the least bit funny but since they wanted to stay out of trouble, they all acted like he was the wittiest guy in the world. Even stupid Frank Gutenkunitz was smiling at him as if Mr. Andriasco were his favorite teacher in all of teacherdom. This is the same Frank Gutenkunitz, mind you, who called Mr. Andriasco "Mole Man" behind his back, because Mr. Andriasco had no chin and a pointy nose and looked like a mole.

"I'm sorry, Mr. Andriasco," I said, hoping he would just give me back my notebook and return to the chalkboard. That was my goal.

Yeah, right, don't hold your breath.

"I'm sorry, too, Mr. MacFarland," he said as he continued to study the drawings in my notebook. "I'm sorry that you've decided not to listen to my factually accurate lesson about evolution in favor of misguidedly dreaming about things that have no basis in scientific fact."

And then, to my horror, he held out my notebook for the whole class to see, as if he were reading a story from a picture book and showing everyone the drawings. They all leaned forward so that they could get a good long look at my most private doodlings, and then they all burst out laughing. I felt like I was going to throw up.

"All right, quiet down," Mr. Andriasco said to the class with a smile that showed he was really pleased with himself. "Mr. MacFarland, I would appreciate it if the only higher form of intelligence you have contact with when you're in my classroom is me." And with that, Mr. Andriasco handed me back my notebook and gave me a look that said I'd be in big trouble if he caught me drawing again. Then he walked back up to the chalkboard.

I looked over and saw Frank Gutenkunitz staring at me. He mouthed the words *MacFartland, you are such a loser* and shook his head to himself, laughing at how stupid he thought I was.

Can I have just *one* good day at school? I thought. Is that asking so much?

Mr. Andriasco picked up his piece of chalk and turned to us. "And for the record, boys and girls, there is no scientific evidence that UFOs even exist. If Mr. MacFarland is waiting around for his alien friends to come and visit him, I'd say he's got a better chance of meeting them by building his own spaceship and flying off to find them himself." He then chuckled at what he thought was a joke and went back to his lecture.

I, however, couldn't concentrate once again. Because I suddenly had something else on my mind. Something really big.

Mr. Andriasco had given me an idea.

# 4

## PATIENCE IS A VIRTUE

The minute we were at our regular cafeteria table, I told my friends Gary and Ivan about my plan.

"All right, you guys," I said, leaning in and talking quietly so that nobody at any nearby tables could hear me. "We're meeting at the barn right after school. We're gonna do something big. Gary, did your brother make his Tennessee fireworks run this month?"

"Uh-huh," said Gary, his mouth full of the really terrible pizza our cafeteria made every Friday afternoon. Everybody always got excited the days our school served pizza, but then everybody always remembered the minute they bit into it that it wasn't good. It always tasted sort of like a big stale saltine cracker with dried-out ketchup and melted-down wax lips on top.

"Bring over as many fireworks as you can," I told him. "Especially bottle rockets."

"But Rick'll kill me if I take his stuff," said Gary as he tried to wash down the hideous pizza with a big drink of chocolate milk that had an expiration date I believe was from the previous decade. Gary's way-older brother, Ricky, was always driving down to Tennessee to buy fireworks because they weren't legal where we lived. The police had even arrested him once for doing it but he just wouldn't stop. I think he was a bit of a pyromaniac. (That's a person who's obsessed with fire, in case you didn't know.)

"This is really important, Gary. Just tell him that the police came and confiscated everything again."

"That's a lie," said Ivan as he chewed on the giant meat-loaf sandwich his mom always sent him to school with. I'd known Ivan ever since we were in kindergarten and I'd never seen him eat anything other than a meat-loaf sandwich at lunch. Gary used to say that when Ivan went to the bathroom, the only thing that came out was a meat-loaf sandwich, which his mom then fished out of the toilet bowl and put back in his lunchbox for the next day. There was only one time Ivan's mom didn't give him a meat-loaf sandwich and that was the day he talked her into packing him a giant

Slim Jim and a Twinkie and nothing else. But then Mrs. Jenkins, the cafeteria guard, came by our table and saw Ivan's lunch and ended up calling his mom and accusing her of being a bad parent.

Anyway, Ivan was pretty religious, so stuff like lying really upset him. He always said that God was just looking for an excuse to punish people. "Are you asking Gary to lie *and* steal at the same time? 'Cause that'll pretty much guarantee that Gary's going to H-E-double toothpicks after he dies."

"Yes, I'm asking Gary to lie and steal, but it's to help *me* out," I said, signaling Ivan to keep his loud voice down. "This is really, *really* important."

Gary and Ivan looked at me, confused. I leaned in even closer to them and whispered really quietly.

"I'm going to build a rocket."

"YOU'RE GOING TO BUILD A *ROCKET?*" Ivan bellowed, loud enough so that people at all the tables around us looked over.

"Shut up!" I whispered, then looked at the people who were staring at us and made a face that was supposed to show them I thought Ivan was crazy and that he had no idea what he was talking about. Then I looked back at him and Gary.

"Tell the whole school, why don't you, loudmouth?" I said to Ivan, who just shrugged and took another bite of his sandwich. When he did, the entire piece of meat loaf slid out the back of the bread slices and dropped onto the table with a splatty-sounding *thud*. I leaned in farther and whispered even quieter this time. "I'm going to build a rocket and fly it into outer space."

They both stared at me.

"What do fireworks have to do with building a rocket engine?" asked Gary.

"What do you think bottle rockets *are?* They're little *rockets*," I said, trying to convince Gary how ignorant he was at that moment. "If we tape a ton of them together, they'll be one *big* rocket. Then all we have to do is stick them on the bottom of the spaceship we're going to build, light them, and I'll go into outer space."

"Uh, Iggy," said Gary. "No offense, but I think you'd better do some more research about rockets."

\*     \*     \*

As much as I hated to admit it, Gary was right.

I *was* an idiot.

It was just that I was so desperate to get to the aliens that I didn't really think things through. I do that a lot. I get excited about something and then I want it right away. My dad always says that's a sign of immaturity but you oughta hear *him* if the waitress at a restaurant doesn't bring his food within five minutes. Then he acts like he hasn't eaten in days and gets all sarcastic with the waitress, saying things like, "What are you doing? Growing the food before you serve it?" and "Oh, I'm sorry, I didn't realize we were in the middle of a famine." Patience is a virtue, my grandma always told my dad when he'd do this, and so I knew that when it came to me and rockets, it was time to get a little more virtuous.

I spent the next week going to the library and looking all over the Internet to learn about rocket engines. I found information from NASA, from rocketry clubs, from college science department Web sites, and from some really old books from the library. My dad always made fun of our local library and said it was more like a book museum, since all the books in it were super old and out of date. But I liked the old books. There was something about them that made me feel good. Maybe it's because they looked like lots of people had read and enjoyed them. For all I knew, inventors and movie stars and famous scientists and presidents could have thumbed through the exact same pages that I was looking through. I thought that was kind of exciting.

Anyway, here's a super fast overview of what I discovered about rockets, since if I tell you all the scientific information I read about, you'll probably fall into a deep sleep from which you will not awaken for centuries.

Okay. Here goes:

There are two kinds of rocket engines. There are liquid propellant engines, and there are solid propellant engines. And liquid propellant engines use liquid fuel and solid propellant engines use solid fuel.

Duh, right?

Now, a solid propellant engine is what I was thinking of when I wanted to use all those fireworks. It's basically a long tube filled with something that's solid and flammable, like the gunpowder that's in a bottle rocket, and there's a hole on one end of the tube. When you light the fuel, it starts to burn really fast, which forces huge flames to shoot out the bottom of the tube, which then push the rocket up off the ground and keep pushing it until it breaks through Earth's atmosphere and away from the gravitational pull of our planet.

Did that make sense?

Well, trust me, it's accurate.

Anyway, when I read about the solid propellant engines, I realized that my plan of taping a bunch of little fireworks together wouldn't work. But I did figure out that if I took all the gunpowder from inside the fireworks and emptied it into one *big* tube and had the tube sticking out the bottom of the spaceship, then I might actually have a shot at getting into outer space when I lit the thing. I just needed to build a spaceship to put the engine on.

And so that's what Gary, Ivan, and I did.

The only problem was we had no idea what we were doing.

# 5

# THREE GARBAGE CANS

Okay, before I tell you all of the stuff I did next, please realize I now know that what I was trying to do was *really* stupid. But at the time it seemed *really* smart. That's the problem with stupid things. They never seem stupid *before* you do them.

Like this rocket I came up with.

I got the idea for it when Ivan and I found these old metal garbage cans under a pile of junk inside his garage. Ivan's garage was majorly disgusting and looked like a fleet of garbage trucks had dumped their entire loads inside of it instead of going to the landfill. Ivan was always saying that his dad was going to clean it out but every weekend we'd see Ivan's dad lying in a lawn chair in his backyard drinking beer and reading magazines that my dad said I wasn't allowed to look at. But the fact that Ivan's dad was such a slob was a good thing for us at that moment, because nobody else in town had metal garbage cans and we couldn't have made a rocket out of plastic ones, which is what all garbage cans are now.

So we grabbed the garbage cans and this huge metal funnel Ivan's dad used to pour oil into his pickup truck's engine and a bunch of other things like nails and tape and hammers and wire and old license plates and wood planks and paint cans and we took it all over to this old abandoned barn in the middle of what we called the dead field.

The dead field was called the dead field because it was, well, dead. That's why there was an old abandoned barn there. Because some poor farmer about a hundred years ago tried to start a farm in the middle of the dead field and then he couldn't get anything to grow. Ever. For his entire life.

Mr. Andriasco told us once that there was some weird blend of mineral deposits in the dirt of the dead field that kept any plants from ever being able to grow there. I always felt sorry for that old farmer a hundred years ago who had pulled a total Ignatius MacFarland by convincing himself he could make a dusty field that had nothing growing in it into something good. I bet there was some other farmer in town who was a jerk like Frank Gutenkunitz who made as much fun of the dead field farmer as Frank made of me all the time. And so I guess I figured that if I could build my rocket in the dead field, maybe somehow I'd be helping that old farmer by turning his farm into a place where something good was finally going to happen.

And so Gary and Ivan and I dumped all the stuff from Ivan's garage in the abandoned barn and got to work building a spaceship. I knew the spaceship had to be big enough for me to get inside. I'd also need room for supplies so that if I got up there and the aliens weren't waiting for me, I wouldn't die of starvation. Plus, I knew I had to have room for all the other stuff that would keep me alive in outer space, like oxygen tanks and computers and control panels that I had no idea how we were going to get.

We cut the bottoms out of two of the garbage cans and wired them onto the other garbage can so that they were stacked three high like the cardboard tube in a roll of paper towels. Then we took the big metal funnel and put it on top, so that the rocket had a pointy nose like all rockets are supposed to have. And then we took a bunch of old license plates that Ivan's dad said he had found in a Dumpster behind the Department of Motor Vehicles and nailed and taped them together to make three fins for the bottom of the rocket. And then we made a door in the side of the garbage cans. After that, we took the boards and built a bunch of little shelves up in the top of the rocket so that I'd have places to put my supplies. And then we lifted the whole rocket onto a bunch of milk crates to get it up high enough off the ground for us to put the engine underneath it — the engine that would send the whole thing and me up into outer space.

After we did all this, we stood back to see just how great our spaceship looked.

Unfortunately, it didn't look very great.

"It looks like something the Little Rascals would have made," Gary said with a frown.

"I don't think it's gonna go into space," said Ivan, who was still chewing on the same piece of beef jerky that he had been chewing on for the past four days. "I don't think it's gonna get two feet off the ground without falling apart."

"Well," I said, trying not to give in to the fact that Gary and Ivan were probably right, "there's only one way to find out."

They stared at me with worried looks as one of the fins fell off and the rocket tipped over.

## COME FLY WITH ME

Gary stole all the fireworks out of the secret locker his brother kept in the tool shed behind his house and brought them over to the barn. There were tons of them — bottle rockets, firecrackers, roman candles, cherry bombs, sparklers, pinwheels — so many that Gary had to cram them all into the soapbox derby car his dad had made when he was a kid (when his *dad* was a kid, which was about four thousand years ago) and then pull the car behind him on his bike, which meant that everybody in our town saw him doing it because when's the last time you saw a kid on a bike pulling a car behind him?

We then spent the next few days doing something that I now realize was totally dangerous and really idiotic, so the fact that I'm telling you about it doesn't mean I think you should do it, too. I'm telling you because what we were doing was so dumb that you should put your hand on your heart and swear in front of a court of law that you'll never do what I'm about to tell you Gary and Ivan and I did. Because I don't want your getting killed to be my fault.

We sat around and carefully cut open all the fireworks and dumped the gunpowder out of them into this big empty paint can. By the time we had gone through all of them, the paint can was filled to the top with the highly explosive and totally dangerous gunpowder.

We then put the lid back on and attached the can upside down to the bottom of the rocket, using a ton of duct tape. I had made a hole in the lid and put one of the long fuses from the fireworks through it so that we could light the engine and then have enough time to get away from it in case huge, kid-burning flames shot out of it when the rocket lifted off. And it was then I realized that, good or not, we had actually done what I had set out to do.

We had made a rocket.

I was desperate to do the test flight right then and there, but it had taken us so long to make the engine that it was dark outside and Gary and Ivan had to go home. So we agreed that we would wait until after school the next day.

I could barely sleep that night, and when I did, I had tons of dreams about the rocket and going into space and all the alien worlds I was going to see and all the extraterrestrial friends I would be making soon. And the next day at school, I couldn't hear anything that any of my teachers said because my head was filled with a million thoughts about how to make a bigger engine and how I would have to convince my cousin Ralph who's been taking scuba diving classes to loan me his oxygen tank so that I'd have a way to breathe in the rocket before the aliens took me onto their spaceship.

And when I had to do my oral report on seeing a Shakespeare play, the only reason I got a halfway decent grade was because I had taken this really expensive old book of the complete works of Shakespeare off my dad's special bookshelf without him knowing it and the teacher was so impressed with it that she didn't realize my report was half as long as it should have been.

I knew that my dad would kill me if he found out I had borrowed his book, because he had always told me that if I was ever reading it and bent even one page, he'd send me off to boarding school and then force me to live with my Aunt Erma, who wasn't even my real aunt. She was just someone my mom had gone to school with whom I had to call Aunt Erma because she wasn't very attractive and was pretty old and hadn't ever gotten married and so she wanted all the kids she knew to call her "aunt" since she didn't have any kids of her own.

I knew I wasn't supposed to take the book but I was so nervous that I'd get an F on my oral report that I figured anything I could do to raise my grade was a good thing. You know, in case my spaceship didn't work and I was stuck here on Earth where things like good grades still counted.

As soon as the bell rang and school was over, I ran out the door so fast that anybody who saw me must have thought my pants were on fire. I got to the dead field so quickly that I ended up having to wait half an hour for Gary and Ivan.

"Thanks for getting here in such a timely fashion," I said super sarcastically when they finally sauntered up holding huge Slurpees in their hands.

"I'm sort of nervous about this, Iggy," said Gary. "What if something goes wrong?"

"You guys, *nothing's* gonna go wrong," I said, trying to get them as excited about this test flight as I was. "This is gonna be great!"

We had decided the previous day that we should try to make the rocket as heavy as it would be if I were inside it. So we found a couple of old cinder blocks in the barn that we stacked on the rocket's floor. But it still didn't seem like it was heavy enough. And that's when I noticed my back-pack, which was filled with all my schoolbooks.

"We can use this," I said as I ran over to the rocket and climbed in. There was barely any room inside it because of the cinder blocks, and so I put my backpack up on one of the shelves we had built in the nose of the rocket.

I then jumped out and closed the door, taping it shut with several pieces of duct tape. Gary and Ivan walked up.

We all stared at the rocket.

"Um . . . what do we do now?" asked Ivan.

"We light the fuse and get far away from it," I said as I pulled out the book of matches I had taken from my dad's barbecue kit.

"Okay," said Gary as he took off running to the barn. "You light it and I'll get far away."

"Yeah," said Ivan, who took off after Gary so fast that he ended up getting to the barn ahead of him. "Good luck, Iggy!"

What a bunch of chickens, I thought. My new alien friends are gonna be way cooler than these guys.

I walked over to the rocket and knelt down to the engine's fuse. I lit a match and, suddenly feeling really nervous and excited and worried and scared and happy, I reached out and lit the fuse. It took a few seconds to start burning, and for a minute I worried that I had put a bad one in. But then sparks flew off the fuse and it started slowly burning up toward the paint can engine.

I turned and ran as fast as I could toward the barn. And when I was almost there, I suddenly realized something.

Something terrible.

Dad's Shakespeare book!

I stopped and saw Gary and Ivan giving me a look that showed they had no idea what I was doing. I then turned and ran as fast as I could back over to the rocket.

"IGGY!" I heard Gary yell. "WHAT ARE YOU DOING?!"

I was running so fast to get there before the fuse burned down to the engine that all I had time to do was wave my hand to tell Gary and Ivan I'd be right back. As I got closer, I saw that the fuse was still burning really slowly. And so I knew I had just enough time to do what I had to do.

I ran up to the rocket and pulled the tape off the door. I then threw the door open and got inside, reaching up to grab my backpack. I got a hold of it but when I pulled it, the shoulder straps got hooked on one of the nails that was holding the shelf in place. I tugged on it but couldn't get it loose. And so I unzipped the bag and tried to dig my hand inside to find the Shakespeare book.

I have to be running out of time, I thought to myself, because even though it didn't feel like I'd been in the rocket very long, sometimes time goes faster than you think when you get busy doing something. And so I had no idea how much more time I had but knew that I had to get out of that rocket right away, Dad's book or no Dad's book.

And that was when it happened.

***KA-BOOOOOOOM!!!***

# THE BARN
# (OR LACK THEREOF)

Completely dazed and totally deaf from the explosion, I crawled out of the rocket. But only after I was able to push open the door, which wasn't easy since the rocket had fallen over on its side, pinning the door shut. I had to rock back and forth to get the rocket to turn over, which I was sure was making Gary and Ivan crack up, seeing the spaceship rolling around like some kind of possessed toilet paper tube. When the door finally fell open, I was never so happy to breathe fresh air in my life. The inside of the rocket was filled with smoke that smelled like somebody had lit a box of pencils on fire, and my eyes were watering like crazy.

I tried to stand up but couldn't. My legs felt like Jell-O and so all I could do was flop onto the ground and lie on my back, coughing and trying to see. I squinted over at the rocket, which didn't look too good. The bottom was smoking like crazy and the explosion of the engine had blown the fins off. The places where we had used wires and duct tape to hold the garbage cans together were all busted open, and smoke was coming out of the cracks. My rocket now looked like a hot dog that somebody had left on the grill too long.

How embarrassing.

I immediately wished that I hadn't done any of this rocket stuff and tried to figure how to get out of there without having to talk to Gary or Ivan, because I could just hear them saying "I told you so!" and "See, we said it wouldn't work!" And if I had to hear them say that after almost getting killed by this stupid rocket we had just built, it was going to be as upsetting as the time I asked Susan Blesnick to the Spring Fling carnival and she said, "Ew, no way."

I rolled over to see if they were coming but no one was there.

"GARY?" I yelled. "IVAN?"

Nothing.

What a couple of jerks, I thought. They're probably laughing so hard that they aren't even able to answer me.

"GARY? IVAN? C'MON, YOU GUYS! HELP ME TAKE THE ROCKET BACK TO THE BARN!"

The last thing I wanted was for Frank Gutenkunitz and his cretin friends to have heard the explosion and then ride over and see my rocket. If I had thought it was bad when Frank found out that my mom had made me take a ballet class at the YMCA when I was five, this would be about ten thousand times worse.

Nobody answered. My ears continued to ring.

"FINE! I'LL DO IT MYSELF!" I said, trying to make them feel guilty.

I started to drag the rocket, but the top came off in my hands.

"ALL RIGHT, FINE! LET'S LEAVE THE STUPID THING HERE! I DON'T CARE."

I took the bottom of my shirt and tried to wipe the water and smoke out of my eyes. It was driving me crazy not to be able to see anything. For all I knew, the entire school could have been standing around the dead field watching me.

When I looked up and was finally able to focus, I tried to see if I could spot Gary and Ivan in front of the barn and quickly noticed one small problem — I couldn't see the barn.

I looked behind me. Then I looked to the left. Then I looked to the right. And finally I turned around in a complete circle.

The barn was gone.

And so were Gary and Ivan.

There was nothing except the field and the trees surrounding it.

Maybe the explosion had destroyed the barn. Maybe the barn got blown away with Gary and Ivan inside. Did I just kill Gary and Ivan? *And* the barn? I tried to find the spot where the barn used to be, but there was nothing. No debris, no Gary, and no Ivan.

I think I'd better go home and tell my parents about this, I said to myself.

And so I headed out of the field.

# A REALLY BAD SUIT OF ARMOR

I couldn't get out of the field.

I don't mean I couldn't walk or anything like that. I mean I couldn't find the path we always took through the trees.

It wasn't there. And there were more trees than usual. And the trees weren't the trees that had been there before. I mean, they *kinda* looked like the trees that had always been there but they weren't the same ones. These trees had round leaves with red and blue veins on them, and the branches were really fat and short, with bark that was pointy and jagged, like the trees were covered with teeth. And they were twice as tall and twice as fat as regular trees and way closer together. Most of the trees were so close that I couldn't see any way to squeeze between them, especially since they were covered with all those pointy thorns.

I'm not going to tell you how many times while I was seeing all this weird stuff I wondered if I was going crazy or if I had a concussion or if I was dead. I kept asking myself if this was heaven or the other *hot* place downstairs (because, after all, I *had* gotten Gary to steal and lie to his brother).

I took out my cell phone, figuring that if I could just talk to my mom then maybe everything would go back to normal. But there was no signal. I tried dialing a few different numbers but nothing went through. Great, I thought. The only reason my parents let me have a cell phone was for emergencies. Well, this pretty much qualified as an emergency. Stupid phone company.

I saw a shadow on the ground about ten feet away from me. It looked like it was from a big bird in the sky above the field. I looked up to see if it was going to be something as weird as the trees and plants I was seeing and quickly realized it was even weirder than I could have imagined. Because it wasn't a bird.

It was a girl.

She was hovering about thirty feet above me, watching me. As soon as I looked up at her, I saw her body flinch, as if she hadn't expected me to notice her. And just like that, she flew away. But my brain took a picture of the flying girl that made it feel like I had just been staring at her for an hour.

She looked like she was about my age, with long hair that was almost white. She seemed really pretty, but it was hard

to tell because there was
something strange-looking about
her, like she was made out of powder or silk or something. I
know that's a pretty weird description, but it's true.

Her arms and legs were longer than most people's, and
the way they floated around her made it look like she was
underwater. Her wings weren't like the wings on a bird.
They were more like two long, skinny bedsheets that floated
like ghosts. Everything about her was more like air and
clouds than skin and muscles and bones. She sure didn't
look like any girl I had ever seen before, especially not any
of the girls that lived around my neighborhood.

After she had flown away, I started running around the
edge of the field, looking for any gap in the trees that I could
squeeze through without shredding myself like a wedge of
Parmesan cheese on a grater. But there were no gaps big
enough. There were several places that were *almost* big

enough, but whenever I tried to get through, the teeth on the trees would be just close enough to grab my shirt and scrape my arms and ears. I was trapped.

I looked over and saw my sad-looking rocket lying on its side in the middle of the field and got an idea. I ran over and started jumping up and down on it, trying to flatten the garbage cans.

When they were almost flat, I stood them back up and squeezed myself and my backpack inside. The garbage cans were now just thin enough for me to push my way sideways through the trees. Or at least thin enough for me to *try* to push through. And trying was better than doing nothing, at that point.

Wearing the cans, I started walking over to the trees, which wasn't easy because I barely had room to move my legs. It was like when you're in the bathroom and you've done a number two but then you see there's no toilet paper and so you have to try to walk to the cabinet to get another roll while your pants are down around your ankles. Well, this was like having your pants wrapped all around your body.

When I got to the trees, I turned sideways and started to push my way through them like a knife cutting through a loaf of bread. The teeth scraping on the sides of the garbage cans sounded like a hundred people were scratching their nails on a chalkboard and I got the shivers so badly I almost peed my pants. I was also sweating like a pig because it was hot inside the cans and I was working so hard to push through the trees that it felt like I was mowing twenty lawns all at once using a lawn mower that didn't have any wheels.

I stopped and tried to catch my breath. It was so tight inside the cans that I couldn't move my arms to wipe off my forehead, which was pouring sweat into my eyes. I felt really trapped and was trying not to freak out.

Just keep going, I told myself.

I took a deep breath and pushed on. All of a sudden, I hit something. I tried to push past but couldn't. I pushed again and moved another couple of inches as the sides of the garbage cans squeezed me like a nutcracker. What if I die? I thought to myself. What if I push again and the cans squeeze me so hard that my heart pops out of my mouth and I croak and then hundreds of years from now when somebody finally cuts down these stupid trees they'll find these two flattened garbage cans with my skeleton inside and say, "Huh . . . I wonder who this kid was and why he was trying to squeeze through these weird trees inside two garbage cans?" And then they'll probably have a good laugh at my expense and toss my bones onto a garbage heap and then tell their friends at dinner that night about the idiot from a hundred years ago who got himself wedged in a bunch of trees for no apparent reason. The thought of this made me so angry that I pushed the garbage cans forward with all my might.

**POP!**

The next thing I knew, I was tumbling head over heels down a hill, my garbage can suit of armor rolling between the trees and banging so hard each time a corner hit the ground that I thought my brains were going to fall out of my head.

Man, am I going to be sore tonight, I thought.

## DATS AND COGS

*BAM! . . . BAM! . . . . . . . . BAM! . . . . . . . . . . . . .*
*. . BAM! . . . . . . . . . . . . . . . . . . . . . . . . BOOM!*

That was what it sounded like inside the garbage cans when I finally slowed and then stopped rolling down the hill. My rocket, which was now more like a square pizza cutter, fell over onto its side with a loud thud. After a few moments of lying there with my head spinning, I grabbed my backpack and pulled myself out.

Nothing looked familiar. Again. Just more weird looking plants and trees. Big things that looked like fat bushes but that had purple leaves and big pointy arms sticking ten feet up in the air. Trees that were growing sideways across the ground with leaves that were about five feet wide and shaped like potato chips. Grass that was orange, with blades that looked more like tongues. And right in the middle of it all was something that looked like a big pile of dirt but that was covered with what appeared to be hundreds of little red watermelons.

I couldn't figure it out. Was I on another planet? I had to be.

And that was when I saw the mouse ears.

The mouse ears were what we all called the two hills that were on the north edge of our town. They were really big, so big that when I was a little kid I used to call them mountains. There was always some rich guy or another coming to our town and looking at the mouse ears because he wanted to turn them into a ski resort in the winter. But then the city council would vote against it because they didn't want tons of ski bums clogging up the streets and having parties all night. Well, according to the position of the mouse ears and the dead field behind me, my neighborhood should have been straight ahead.

But it wasn't.

There wasn't anything except more weird-looking plants as far as I could see.

I spent the next few hours walking through what I was certain used to be my neighborhood, but every place where I knew a house or store or building should have been no longer had a house or store or building there. Just more weird plants and trees and nothing even remotely resembling the town in which I grew up. I kept checking my cell phone but there was still no signal, only an X where it normally showed how strong the reception was. Cellular technology was clearly not going to be of any use to me here.

Now, I don't want to make it sound like I was just walking around going, "Oh, that's interesting. Hmm. My hometown is no longer here. What a funny thing." I wasn't tapping my chin thoughtfully with my finger while pondering the disappearance of everything I had ever known, talking to myself like some English guy in one of those movies about the old British colonies in India, going, "I say, that's a bit odd, all my friends and family nowhere to be seen. I think I'll have a spot of tea and think about this for a while." No, I was really freaking out.

Like, if you could see a picture of me during all this, my mouth was probably hanging open so wide that a vast assortment of bugs and birds could have flown in and built several nests and laid mountains of eggs in my teeth. I don't want to say that I started to cry at one point, because that would be kind of embarrassing. So let's just say that I was in shock.

Thank you for your discretion.

When I got to the river that ran through what *used* to be the middle of town, I heard a weird noise. I turned around and saw this strange-looking dog sitting up in a tall tree. First of all, the dog had a really wide nose, like he had gotten two noses for the price of one. Next, his coat was made of really long brown fur that was striped with white lines. And finally, he was licking his paw and wiping his face with it over and over, the same way Gary's cat always did. And the fact that the dog was sitting way up in a tree seemed a bit, well . . . odd.

As I was staring at it, the dog looked down at me for a few seconds, and then went back to licking its paws, as if I didn't exist.

Dogs usually like me. I'm always the person who gets jumped on and has his face licked. My mom says it's because I'm a nice person, but then my dad tells her that dogs just lick people to get the salt off them. But even with all the sweating I had just done getting those garbage cans through the trees and then walking for two hours while I dealt with the fact that everything I knew no longer existed, I apparently still wasn't sweaty enough to motivate a weird-looking dog to come out of a tree and say hello.

As I stared at the dog, I heard a really loud and deep

meow. I turned around to see a cat running toward me. It wasn't much bigger than a normal house cat, but it had ears that were really long and pointy and eyes that were way bigger than usual. I didn't know if the cat was going to attack me or not. But it was coming so fast, all I could do was stand there.

The cat jumped against my leg and stood on its back feet, its tail wagging wildly and its tongue hanging out like a dog's. I reached down to pet it and it started licking my hand like crazy. And then, before I even knew what was happening, the cat spotted the dog sitting up in the tree. It meowed like it wanted to kill the dog and raced over. It started jumping up and down, meowing louder and louder as the dog stood up and arched its back and began hissing at the cat.

All I could do was stand there and wonder what I'd gotten myself into when I built that rocket.

Well, *you* wanted to escape, I told myself.

Mission accomplished.

If only I knew what the fudge was going on. (Yes, I said "fudge." What's it to you?)

# 10

# GALLONS OF PEE

I figured I should keep walking along the river, since I had learned in social studies class that all towns and cities are built where there's water.

And so I walked. For miles.

The cat who thought it was a dog ran along beside me. It kept stopping and lifting its leg to pee on pretty much every plant we passed and, quite frankly, it was starting to make me feel like barfing. It's not that seeing animals go to the bathroom makes me sick, but this cat seemed to let loose with about a gallon of pee every time it went. It sounded like someone was shooting a garden hose into the ground every five seconds. I kept trying to get away from the cat but as soon as I started to leave it would come tearing after me through the grass so fast you would have thought my pockets were filled with catnip or fish or something.

Up one hill, down another. Up another hill, down yet another. Hours passed. I'd never walked so much in my life. I was hungry, I was tired, and I felt completely lost. So when the cat unloaded another truckload of pee onto a bush, I suddenly lost it and yelled, "STOP PEEING ON EVERYTHING! YOU'RE MAKING ME SICK!"

The cat stopped and looked at me. Did it understand what I said? Maybe it was smarter than I thought.

"Um . . . is there a town around here?" I asked it, immediately feeling like a moron for talking to a cat.

The cat suddenly started jumping up and down, its tongue hanging so far out of its mouth that it looked like it was choking on a big pink stick of chewing gum.

"Am I going the right way?"

The cat jumped up and down again, then spun in a circle. Maybe it *does* understand me, I thought.

"A town?" I asked, getting excited because the cat was getting excited. "A town with people?"

The cat looked like its head was going to explode, and then it suddenly tore off into a dense wall of trees. Is the town through there? I wondered. And am I going to have to go back and put on those stupid, hot, sweaty garbage cans again?

Before I could ponder this too long, the cat burst out of the trees with a big stick in its mouth. It ran up and dropped the stick at my feet, then looked up at me to see if I would throw it.

Great. Stupid cat.

I picked up the stick and threw it over the hill as hard as I could. The cat tore after it as if it were trying to make the game-winning catch in the final inning of the Feline World Series.

After a few seconds, I heard tons of angry meowing, as if some sort of cats-who-think-they're-dogs fight had just broken out. I ran up the hill to see what was going on and there, spreading out before me in the valley below, was a huge city. It was way bigger than any city I had ever seen and definitely bigger than any city that existed anywhere near where I lived.

I couldn't really stare at the city too long, though, because the cat-who-thought-it-was-a-dog was in a huge fight with a bunch of other cats-who-thought-they-were-dogs because they all wanted that stupid stick I had just thrown. I suddenly got nervous that the cat who had been following me was actually going to get hurt. It's not that I liked the cat or anything. But since it was I who had thrown the stick, I sort of felt responsible for it.

I ran down to where the cats were fighting and started yelling and clapping my hands to scare them away. "HEY!

KNOCK IT OFF!" I yelled as the cats all scattered. I picked up my cat to see if it was hurt, which proved to be a bad idea because it immediately peed all down the front of my shirt.

I don't think it meant to do it, because it then started licking my face like crazy, like it was saying thank you or something. And fortunately it seemed like cat pee in this weird place didn't really stink the way it usually does in my grandma's house. But the fact of the matter was I now had a shirt that was soaked with cat pee.

This has not been a good day so far, I thought. But at least I found a city with people in it who can tell me what's going on.

Well, I was sorta right.

# 11

# WELCOME TO LESTERVILLE. NOW GO HOME.

The minute the cat and I came down toward the city, I could tell things were not going to get any more normal.

The first thing that happened was I almost killed myself. I was walking and looked back to see if the cat was still following me, and I fell right into a hole. I'm not talking about a small hole, either. I mean a *big* hole, about three feet wide. Fortunately, there was some sort of ancient-looking door about two feet down inside it that kept me from going into the bowels of the earth. I crawled out and noticed that there were tons of holes all over the place. From the way the plants and trees had grown around them, they looked like they had been there forever.

The cat and I walked through the neighborhood of holes and eventually came to the actual city. "Welcome to Lesterville!" a big sign read.

At first, the buildings were very old and odd. They all looked like different-sized igloos that were made out of weathered clay and stone, with some kind of see-through material covering the windows. There were colorful heavy cloth awnings sticking out over the windows and some of the buildings had big windmills on top of them. The doors and windows on the buildings were round, too, and so were the ancient-looking decorations that were painted on the sides of everything.

The streets also seemed to be based on circles, since they all curved around, making it hard to look very far down any road without seeing more buildings. It was a bit nerve-racking because I couldn't see if anyone was heading down a street toward me. For some reason, though, everything seemed to be deserted. The only sound I could hear was the breeze making the awnings flap and the windmills squeak as they turned. Lesterville is a pretty boring old place, I thought.

The cat and I kept walking through the winding streets, seeing every size and style of round building that Lesterville had to offer. Some were really big, and some were so small, only one person could fit inside at a time. I started to wonder if maybe the small ones were like little bathrooms. And the more I thought about bathrooms, the more I had to *go* to the bathroom. I mean, like, really bad.

I thought about maybe just finding an alley and sneaking into it and doing a number one without a toilet, but there were no alleys and I didn't want to just go in the street. But pretty soon, I knew I was either going to have to go to the bathroom in a place where I might be seen, or go in my pants. And since my shirt was already covered with cat pee, the thought of then having my pants soaked with my *own* pee was not really an attractive option.

And that was when I saw it.

A coffee shop!

I almost fainted. It was a Starbucks, and yet it wasn't a Starbucks. It was called Artbucks, even though it had the exact same sign and logo that a Starbucks has. It even looked like a Starbucks, except that it was ... well ... really terrible.

I don't mean it was dirty or scary or run-down. It looked really new. But it also looked like somebody who didn't know how to build a Starbucks had built it. It wasn't round like all the other buildings I had seen so far. It was square, just like the Starbucks in my hometown. It had the same Starbucks windows and doors and tables and chairs, but it looked like the people who built it didn't have a clue what they were doing. The windows and doors were all crooked, the tables looked really wobbly, and the legs on the chairs were all different lengths. The writing on the sign was uneven, and the logo looked like a five-year-old had drawn it.

Still, the place looked like paradise to me, because I knew that there had to be a bathroom inside. I started to head toward it but realized that the cat had stopped. Not that I needed a cat with me to take a number one, but since it had followed me everywhere else so far, it made me nervous that it was just sitting there.

"Are you coming or not?" I asked it.

The cat meowed and then took off running down the street.

Either the cat was afraid of coffee or else it knew something I didn't. However, since it had the luxury of being able to pee anywhere it pleased and I didn't, I ran to the Artbucks and went in.

And that's when things got reeeeeeeeeeeally weird.

How weird?

Well, let's just say the second I was in, I completely forgot that I had to go to the bathroom, because there in front of me was the weirdest scene I had ever witnessed in my life.

The place was packed. But it wasn't packed with people. It was filled with the strangest assortment of creatures I had ever laid eyes on in my life.

Closest to me, there were two creatures that kind of looked like huge six-foot-tall moles with flippers sticking out of their chests and backs. They had two really thick legs that looked like hairy logs, and instead of their legs being side by side like normal legs are, they were front and back. So when they walked their front leg would extend out and their back leg would push off. And this meant that they walked really slowly, like their bodies had never been intended to move this way in the first place.

Their flippers each had a big super sharp-looking claw on the end, and their faces, which were on top of their heads, had long black noses that stuck straight into the air. They didn't have any eyes that I could see, and their bodies were covered with thick, tough-looking brown hair.

Well, that is, the parts of their bodies that weren't covered by their clothes.

As weird as it sounds, they were wearing big polo shirts and flowery Hawaiian shorts, with what I think were supposed to be flip-flops on their feet. However, since they didn't really have toes, the flip-flops were barely hanging on to the little claws around each foot. So every time they'd step forward, they'd have to bring their foot back and retrieve their flip-flop, since it kept falling off.

One of them was trying to carry a cup of coffee it had just bought, but its flippers weren't able to come together enough to get a good grip on it. And so it was having a really hard time keeping the cup steady, which meant that coffee was spilling all down the front of its shirt as it tried to walk. The other mole creature grabbed its cup off the counter, but its claw went through the side of the cup and hot coffee squirted out all over the floor. They were like some otherworldly comedy team, although I don't think either of them found the situation funny.

That was my introduction to the mole guys. But, as my dad used to say, they were only the tip of the iceberg.

There were four creatures standing in line behind the mole guys that sort of looked like a cross between fish and eels (Karen called them *feels*, which I guess is better than calling them ee-ishes, but since you haven't even met Karen yet, I'll stop bringing up her name). They were about five feet tall with slippery-looking skin that turned different colors when the light hit it. They each had one big black eye, a long thin mouth, and an "arm" with a big suction cup on the end coming out of their backs.

One of the feels was sticking and unsticking its suction cup on the counter impatiently as it glared at the really slow creature working the cash register, while another feel tugged at the collar of the sweater it was wearing. They all had on different colored turtle-necks that went down to the part of their bodies that were coiled on the ground and they used their coils to slither across the floor, which made it almost look like they were floating.

The creature that was working the cash register and getting the feel's angry suction cup–popping directed at it looked like a fat four-foot-tall weasel with one eye and three arms.

Right then, another creature that looked like a leathery fox stuck its head out from the back room and yelled something I couldn't understand. The weasel looked over, couldn't see the fox because another creature that looked like what I can only describe as a giant eight-foot-tall purple baby with five arms and tiny eyes was in the way, and all of a sudden the weasel's body expanded straight up like it had a spring inside it. And then it just looked like a really tall, skinny weasel that didn't actually look like a weasel at all because of its big yellow eye and its three arms and the fact that its head wasn't really shaped like a weasel's head, anyway.

All right, look. I'm sorry if this all sounds really confusing and bizarre, but this stuff is super hard to explain. I mean, it's not like I ever got As and Bs in English class. And it's not like I had a camera with me during all this because my dad refused to let me have a cell phone with a camera in it because he said they were stupid. Anyway . . .

The creature that was making the coffee drinks didn't seem to know what it was doing. It looked like a five-foot-tall praying mantis with lots of twiggy arms that it was using to make a bunch of drinks at once. But as it worked the huge espresso machine (that looked like the world's biggest piece of junk and had steam coming out from a million different cracks and gaps), the bug kept spilling the drinks and overfilling the cups and dumping coffee grounds into the milk that was all gray and looked totally gross. And then every creature that got their drink from the bug would either drop it on the ground because the cup was too hot or try to drink it and burn its mouth or drink it and then make a face like it was the worst-tasting thing ever, and it was at that moment I couldn't help but think maybe having an Artbucks in Lesterville wasn't such a good idea.

Sitting around at the tables were other creatures of all shapes and sizes that kinda looked like animals and kinda looked like people and yet didn't look like either one. I had seen in tons of science fiction movies and TV shows that while aliens always looked different than people did on Earth, they still had two arms and two legs and two eyes and a nose and a mouth like we all do. And that's why I was so freaked out when I saw these creatures.

It seemed like somebody had tossed a bunch of body parts from every type of animal and person in the world into a box, tossed in a bunch of other weird stuff, and shook it up and whatever dumped out each time they tipped the box over would become some living thing. It was like being in a whole different reality, except for the fact that we were standing in a Starbucks that was called Artbucks and that the creatures were all wearing poorly fitting clothes that looked like what all my friends back home wore.

The reason I haven't mentioned what they were saying was that I couldn't *hear* what they were saying. It wasn't that they weren't making noise. It was because there was really loud music playing that was drowning them out. But it wasn't weird alien creature music.

It was Frank Sinatra.

The reason I knew this was my dad is a huge Frank Sinatra fan and so we always had his music playing in our house, so much so that my mom would constantly tell my dad if he put on one more Frank Sinatra song she was going to divorce him. But then he'd put on another one and my mom would laugh and then they'd get up and dance and kiss and it would have been really sweet if it was in a movie and it wasn't my parents doing it, which simply made it gross and disturbing.

But that's why I can tell you that even though Frank Sinatra was playing in the coffee shop, it wasn't *actually* Frank Sinatra that was playing in the coffee shop.

It was a recording of somebody who *wished* he was Frank Sinatra.

The music was really strange and was coming out of a bad sound system and sounded like the musicians on the record were playing toy instruments they had made in wood shop. The songs were close to being Frank Sinatra songs, but the words and the music weren't quite right. It was like they were being performed by someone who couldn't remember exactly how they went and so they just played them the way they thought they were supposed to go. And I can tell you that whoever was playing must have had a terrible memory.

But the worst part was the singer. His voice was really bad and out of tune, and he had the words all wrong. Which would have been okay but since he was the world's worst singer, it was a pretty bad combination. I mean, I sing badly, but this guy made me sound like ... well ... Frank Sinatra.

I was so stunned by everything I was seeing and hearing that I was just standing there in the doorway even though I still had to go to the bathroom.

And that was when all the creatures in the Artbucks turned and looked at me.

They all gasped like they had just seen a ghost and I gasped like a ghost that had just been seen and before I knew what I was doing, I was running down the street away from the coffee shop, since I didn't know if these creatures were friendly or were going to eat me. I ran around the corner looking for a place to hide and suddenly found myself in what looked like the center of town. And despite how scared I was and how much I wanted to hide, I stopped again and stared in disbelief.

And, trust me, you would have, too.

# 12

## THE PLAY'S THE THING

Have you ever been to New York City?

If not, there's a place there called Times Square, and it's this super huge town center where a bunch of streets come together and there's tons of stores and big billboards and neon signs and cars and people and it looks like the craziest place on earth.

I've never been there but I've seen it a bunch on TV because every New Year's Eve they have a party there and thousands of people come out and watch them lower this big lighted ball. When it gets to the bottom of the pole everybody yells "Happy New Year!" and they kiss and hug and then it's officially the next year.

Well, the reason I stopped running and stood there staring was that I was suddenly standing in Times Square.

Or what *looked* like Times Square.

A really terrible version of Times Square.

There were no old round buildings anywhere. They had all been replaced with new ones that were supposed to look like the buildings in the real Times Square. But just like the coffee shop looked like it was made by people who didn't know what they were doing, these buildings looked like they were made by people who *really* didn't know what they were doing. There were skyscrapers that were as crooked as chewed-up drinking straws, and they creaked and swayed whenever the slightest breeze blew. The lower buildings were close to caving in, and the creatures I could see through the windows walked slowly and nervously, like they knew that if they walked too fast they'd cause the place to collapse.

Occasionally a big piece of roof would fall off one of the skyscrapers and smash down onto the street, sending the creatures on the sidewalks running in all directions. There were big, poorly painted signs everywhere advertising poorly built stores and restaurants and places and products that I had seen tons of times on TV and in magazines, but now they all had different names.

McDonalds was McArthurs. Coca Cola was now Artha Cola. An ad for what looked like Disneyland said it was called Arthneyland. There was a big billboard for the new *Arthur Potter* book written by someone named J. K. Arthling. There was a Crate and Arthur, an Arthurcrombie and Fitch, an Arthurs Sonoma, a J.C. Artheys, and a store called Art that looked a lot like a Gap. There was even an underwear store called Arthur's Secret.

The street signs read Sixth Artvenue, Seventh Artvenue, and Eighth Artvenue. The movie theaters were showing *Art Wars*, *The Artpire Strikes Back*, *Return of the Arti*, *Art of the Rings*, *Gone With the Art*, *Raiders of the Lost Art*, *The Artfather, Parts I and II*, and *SpiderArt*. There was an Art Central Station, a Madison Square Arthurs, an Artpire State Building, an Arthurgie Hall — there was even a Museum of Modern Art Art.

And it all looked really wrong.

There were creatures all over the place. And they were lumbering or slithering or hopping or crawling or rolling or oozing around the square as they shopped in the stores and ate in the restaurants and looked at the buildings and sat on the benches and acted just like the people I had always seen in all the pictures and movies and TV shows about New York.

The only thing that didn't exist in any of the pictures I had ever seen of Times Square was a gigantic sign that was now standing right in the middle of everything, written in letters that were about twenty feet high, that read:

# Artlish Only!

It was right then that a really loud bell rang three times. All the creatures stopped when they heard it, and then started running immediately in the same direction. I looked around in a panic. There must be some kind of an attack coming, I thought, waiting for the arrival of an invading army or fighter jets or who knows what, since everything I'd seen so far had been weirder than anything I could have imagined.

But nothing happened.

The creatures all kept running and then disappeared down Seventh Artvenue. Then there was nothing but silence. Seeing that nobody was in the square and seconds from peeing my pants, I quickly jumped behind a big garbage can and finally took the whiz that had been making my back teeth float for the last half hour.

As I relieved myself, all I could think about was how Ivan's dad once got a ticket for public urination when the police caught him going to the bathroom behind a Chuck E. Cheese after he drank four huge Cokes at Gary's birthday party and went out the wrong door looking for the men's room. I suddenly wondered if a Lesterville police creature was going to appear out of nowhere and take me to some kind of jail that would be ten times stranger than the Art-

bucks. Not that they'd be wrong to. I mean, peeing anywhere other than a bathroom is a pretty terrible thing to do
unless you happen to be out in the middle of the woods. I
wasn't proud of myself. But I have to say that I sure felt a
whole lot better after I did it. Like my uncle Lou used to
say, "When you gotta go, you gotta go."

I finished my business and started walking cautiously down the sidewalk, which was completely cracked and had holes all over the place. Now that I had gone to the bathroom, I was really hungry. So as I walked past the McArthurs, I took a deep breath to see if I could smell the hamburgers. I immediately started coughing and choking because the smell coming out of the place was more like somebody had just taken a huge dump in there than the smell of a place where hamburgers were being made. When I looked back at Seventh Artvenue, I saw that the creatures were lining up for something right around the corner. Curious, I kept walking forward to see what they were waiting for.

There, at the front of the line, was a big theater. The creatures were heading in to see a show. And when I looked up at the marquee to see what was playing, I saw something written on it that I never expected to see in a million years:

## HAMLET

You know . . . the play by William Shakespeare? The play we had seen the high schoolers perform and that was the reason why I brought my dad's really expensive old book to class? The book that was the reason I ran back inside the rocket right before it exploded and brought me to this weird place? All these strange new creatures I never knew existed before were going to see this really good but hard to understand play about a prince in Denmark who finds out that his father was murdered and then tries to avenge his death.

Pretty weird, right? Well . . .

Was this what I was so surprised about when I saw that marquee? Would you believe me if I told you it wasn't?

Well, you'd better because the thing that surprised me the most was that written under the word "Hamlet" it read:

## A new play written by our president and leader, His Most Royal Excellency, Chester L. Arthur

And next to this was a picture of Chester L. Arthur, who was none other than . . .

Mr. Arthur, the English teacher from my school who was killed five years ago when his house blew up!

I was so shocked to see it that I forgot where I was and started to walk toward the sign, trying to figure out just what the heck was going on.

And that was when somebody tackled me.

# 13

## KAREN . . . FINALLY

Actually, the word "tackled" is probably too polite.

- Knocked me down and almost killed me.
- Hit me so hard that I thought my head was going to come off.
- Creamed me into the ground and smashed me as flat as a pancake.

However you want to phrase it, I was practically knocked unconscious. And it scared the you-know-what out of me. For all I knew, I was about to be eaten by some weird tiger-like creature that had fins instead of paws or a giant walking oyster with a mouth full of razor sharp teeth. As I closed my eyes and prepared to find out what it feels like to be eaten alive, I heard a voice whisper angrily in my face, "What are you trying to do? Get yourself *killed?!*"

It wasn't some weird creature's voice and it wasn't one of my friends' voices, since I thought that maybe I was having one of those moments like you always see in movies where someone thinks something bad is happening to them but then it turns out that they were asleep and the voice of who-ever was about to hurt them turns into the voice of one of their friends trying to wake them up. No, this wasn't either of those things.

This was a girl's voice.

I opened my eyes to see Karen. Only, I didn't know she was Karen at that moment. I didn't know she was Karen be-cause I didn't *know* Karen at that moment. When I opened my eyes and saw her, all I knew was that a sixteen-year-old girl who had long black hair and kind of a pretty face was sitting on top of me with her nose about half an inch from mine and that she was really mad.

"What do you think you're doing, walking around and letting everybody see you?" she hissed in my face like Gary's cat used to do whenever I would try to touch its paws. "Are you really that *stupid*, kid?"

And with that, she looked back toward the theater where Mr. Arthur's *Hamlet* was playing, then grabbed me by the front of my shirt and dragged me off into the alley. She was pulling me so fast and so hard that I couldn't stand up.

"You're ripping my pants!" I said as she dragged me along the rock-covered ground. Sort of weird to think that those were the first words I ever said to Karen. But, well, she *was* ripping my pants.

"Shut up!" she whispered loudly.

Before I could say another word, she stopped, pulled open a small door at the end of the alley that was hidden behind a pile of garbage, and shoved me inside it headfirst. To do this, she grabbed my belt buckle and used it like a handle, so that as she pushed me into the doorway she gave me such a monstrous wedgie that I was sure I would be talking in a soprano voice for the rest of my life.

"OW—!" I said as she clapped her hand over my mouth and pushed me the rest of the way in. Then she scrambled in after me and pulled the door shut with a *slam!*

Before I could figure out where I was, she sat on top of my chest again and stuck her face in my face, like she was a police interrogator. "How did you get here?"

"You just pushed me in!" I knew exactly what she meant but since she was being so mean to me, I sort of felt like not being the most cooperative person in the world. I'm not a fan of mean people.

"How did you get to *this world,* you stupid kid?" I could tell that she knew I knew what she was talking about and it only seemed to make her madder that she had to ask me again. As far as first meetings go, ours was not going well.

"Why are you being such a jerk?" I asked.

"Why are *you* being such a baby?" she asked back.

"Get off me! You're crushing my ribs."

"Man, you're a wuss."

"Hey, shut up. I don't even know you."

"Thank God."

"What's that supposed to mean?"

"It means that the only reason I bothered to save you was that if they caught you they'd probably use you to get to me!"

"What are you talking about?" I asked, since I was pretty confused at that point. "Who wants to catch me?"

"Yeah, like you don't know."

"I don't! I have no idea where I am or what's going on or why everything I've been seeing for the past four hours is completely different from anything I've ever seen in my life! So stop yelling at me and get your butt off my chest!"

She gave me a weird look like I had said something that surprised her, then sat up so that she wasn't in my face anymore, even though she was still sitting on me and crushing my rib cage.

"Four hours?" she said, shocked. "Do you mean you *just* got here?"

"Yes!" It's pretty embarrassing to admit but when I said this I was sort of about two seconds away from crying. Not that I'm the kind of kid who starts crying if anything bad happens. I'd had plenty of bad stuff happen to me over the years but very seldom did I cry about it. I mean, I wasn't like Paul Fresco, the big tall kid who was a grade higher than me who was famous for crying whenever anything happened to him. He even started crying once just because somebody asked him why he always cried.

"How did you get here?" she asked.

"I told you, I don't know. My friends and I made a rocket but the engine exploded when I went inside it and when I got out of it, everything was gone and I was wherever this place is."

I was trying really hard to hold it together but my stupid nose was starting to run and so I had to do a big sniffle the second I finished what I said. Fortunately, she seemed to be thinking about something else and wasn't really paying attention to me or my nose at that moment.

"Then it's true," was all she said, way more to herself than to me.

"What's true?" I asked with another big embarrassing sniffle.

"That's the same way I got here," she said, looking at me like I was supposed to be all amazed.

"You built a rocket and it blew up?"

"No, dummy, I got here because of an explosion, too."

"You did?" I asked, pretending to scratch my nose while actually intercepting a drip that was about to come out. "What kind of explosion?"

"I was mixing a bunch of chemicals that I wasn't supposed to be mixing in my chemistry class and the whole thing exploded and when I woke up, I was lying on top of a hill next to this city."

I was pretty surprised when she told me this, I have to admit, because it made me remember something. A year ago, there was this big story in our local paper about this weird girl from the high school who had blown herself up in science class. I didn't know who she was, but the kids in my grade with older brothers and sisters said she was this really strange girl who was pretty smart but who never talked to anybody and who always dressed like she thought she was living in a vampire movie. A lot of people thought that she blew herself up on purpose because she only listened to really depressing music about death and dying. It always sounded a lot to me like the way Mr. Arthur had died. Or appeared to have died, since both his and Karen's bodies were never found at the explosion sites.

"I read about you in the newspaper. Everybody thinks you blew yourself up on purpose," I said, wondering if she was going to get mad.

She did.

"God, that's so stupid! Figures all those mindless drones in that toilet of a town would think I would kill myself just because I wasn't one of them. Yes, that's me. The poor little suicidal freak." She glared at me like I was the one who had started the rumor about her. Although I guess I *was* sort of guilty because when I had read about her, I just assumed that the story was true. Still . . .

"Hey, don't get mad at me. I wasn't the one who said you did it. I don't even know you," I said defensively. "If it makes you feel any better, everybody thinks that Mr. Arthur killed himself, too."

"He did kill himself," she said, giving me a look that showed she thought I was a moron. "Or he thought he did. Too bad he didn't."

"What are you talking about?" I asked, a bit put off that she had just wished Mr. Arthur dead. "What's going on? How did we all get here?"

"Don't you get it?" she said with another you're-an-idiot look. "We jumped *frequencies*."

I was completely confused.

"Don't stare at me like you just smelled dog poop," she said. "Look. Each one of us was caught in an explosion. Each one of us ended up here. Our explosions knocked us into a parallel reality."

"What's that mean?"

"It means we're existing in the same space on the same planet as the one we knew back home, but we're in a different frequency of it. Like when you press the button on a car stereo to change the station. The music is coming out of the same radio in the same car, but it's completely different because it's at a different frequency."

I looked at her like I thought she was crazy but quickly realized that what she was saying sort of made sense. But it didn't make it any easier to understand.

"How do you know this?" I asked, trying to use a nice tone of voice so that she wouldn't yell at me again.

"I just know it, okay? Think about it. When you got out of your rocket, were you in the same place you were before the explosion? Were you surrounded by the same mountains and hills and stuff?"

She was right. The dead field was still the dead field after the explosion and the mouse ears were still where they had been back home. Only the barn was gone. Although . . .

"Wait a minute. All the trees and plants and grass were different. So it wasn't really the same place," I said, feeling smart.

"No duh, genius," she said sarcastically (as if you couldn't tell). "That's all the *living* stuff. The plants and everything evolved differently here than it did back where we're from. But the hills and the mountains and the whole planet are the same. Like after I woke up from the explosion, I was on top of a hill. And it was the same hill that the high school is built on top of. It's just that the school doesn't exist in this reality. Thank God."

I tried to take this all in but was feeling a bit overwhelmed. "What do you mean, that the living things evolved differently?"

"What grade are you in?" she asked with the same I-just-smelled-dog-poop look she had yelled at me for having on my face moments earlier.

"Seventh," I said defensively.

"Don't they teach you about evolution in science class?" Then she gave me a weird look. "You don't go to some crazy private school, do you?"

"No, I go to the same junior high you went to. And I *know* about evolution." I was suddenly kicking myself for all the alien drawings I had made while Mr. Andriasco was giving his lectures about evolution, as well as hoping that she wouldn't ask me to explain it.

"Yeah?" she said as she arched her eyebrow at me. "Then what is it?"

Great.

"It's . . . uh . . . it's . . . um . . . uh . . ." Man, I should have paid more attention in class.

"You're the reason that schools are losing funding, kid," she said with a smirk. "Evolution means that everything develops from a really basic form. And since this is a different world, everything in it developed and evolved differently than in our world."

"How's that possible?"

"The only reason things look the way they do in our world is because of billions of tiny mutations that happen over millions of years. It's all random and can come out differently every time. Some single cell creatures develop into multiple cell creatures. Then while they're all multiplying and having kids, one or two of their kids have a different gene in their DNA that makes them stronger or more able to survive than the others. So those plants and creatures live while the other ones die and the stronger ones multiply again.

"Eventually, they or their kids or their kids' kids have some kids who have a mutated gene that makes *them* stronger and more able to survive. So those become the new creatures and on and on for millions of years until suddenly everything looks either the way it does here or in that stupid town we used to live in."

"What do you mean 'used to'?" I said, probably sounding way more scared and whiny than I wanted to in front of her.

"I mean that if you know some way for us to get back there, I'd love to hear it. Because I can tell you from a year's worth of experience that we are majorly trapped in this frequency."

"Can't we just make another explosion and get back?"

"You think I haven't tried that? How do you think I got all of Arthur's whack pack after me?"

"Whack pack? What's Arthur's whack pack?" I really hate when I don't know stuff and so I end up saying "What?" and "Huh?" and "What are you talking about?" during a whole conversation. Usually I'll just pretend that I know what people are referring to and then go home and check on the Internet to figure out what it was I was pretending to understand. But at this moment, I couldn't understand anything Karen was talking about and I didn't have any Internet to run home to because I didn't *have* a home anymore.

"Trust me, kid," she said with a serious look. "You'll find out."

And that was when the wall on the other side of the room exploded.

# 14

## I AM OF ABSOLUTELY
## NO HELP AT ALL

Karen screamed and I screamed even louder as a cloud of dust blew all over us and rocks and all kinds of other junk rained down from the explosion. I had so much dust in my eyes that I couldn't see what was going on at first.

But then I could. And suddenly I wished I couldn't.

Through all the dust and smoke I saw really bright light pouring through the hole in the wall that the explosion had made. And through the hole I suddenly saw about five or six big creatures walk into the room. The first one through was one of the mole guys, which meant he was walking really slowly. But he wasn't dressed in a Hawaiian shirt and shorts like the ones at Artbucks had been. This one was wearing some kind of army uniform. And he looked really mean.

His body was bigger and bulkier than the Artbucks mole guys, and when he looked at Karen and me with his long pointy nose, I saw that his face had what seemed to be a really nasty expression on it. (Though it was hard to tell with the mole creatures, since their faces weren't really like faces that you and I are used to seeing.) He was carrying a huge sword/ax weapon that immediately became even scarier to me than he was. He stopped when he saw Karen and me and said in a really deep and hard-to-understand voice, "I knew I smelled them!"

As the other creatures came into the room, all dressed in their army uniforms, I quickly realized that as big as the huge mole guy was, he was small compared to the rest of them. I recognized another creature as one of the huge five-armed purple babies. But this one looked like the meanest baby in the world. And since it was holding a huge spear with the most deadly-looking pitchfork thing on the end, you can see I'm not exaggerating when I say it was the nastiest-looking infant ever.

Next to the baby was one of the praying mantis creatures, like the one that had been making coffee at the Artbucks. But where that bug creature was skinny like a stick, this bug was as big as the huge hundred-year-old log that we had lying in our backyard. Instead of having twiggy arms, its arms were thick and spiky and each one was holding a big square knife blade that would flash a bright glint right into my eyes when any light hit its super sharp-looking edges.

The rest of the creatures coming into the room were kinds I hadn't seen before. One looked like a six-foot-tall hairy rolled-up potato bug with an arm sticking out one side and a tentacle with what I guess was its eyeball sticking out the other. It rolled through the hole in the wall and was holding this spinning weapon that looked like a wagon wheel with blades stuck all over it. Another creature was like a giant four-legged walking octopus with what looked like a fly's eye for a head. Strapped onto the front of each of its feet was a block with sharp metal spikes sticking out.

When the giant octopus creature saw Karen and me (or is it Karen and I? — I can never remember), it lifted one of its blocks of spikes and pointed it right at us, like it was telling us it was going to kill us as soon as it was allowed to. A couple of other creatures were coming in behind these but before I could focus on them, Karen stood up and blocked my view.

"Get out of here, dirt-eater!" Karen yelled at the mole guy as she reached over with one hand and grabbed a long bamboo-looking pole that was leaning against the wall. Oh, great, I thought, that pole's really gonna protect us against the knives and spikes and blades that just arrived in the room.

"You are under arrest for trying to destroy Lesterville," the mole guy said in his deep, rumbling voice. When he did, all the other creatures growled or hummed or snorted or made some other weird sound that said they didn't like Karen and that the chances were very good they weren't going to like me, either.

"You're as stupid as your president, you know that?" Karen said with a laugh. "Lesterville doesn't need me to destroy it. All it'll take is one good gust of wind."

"Hey," I whispered loudly to her, since I still didn't know her name at that moment. "Don't make them mad."

"Too late," said the mole guy. He then turned to the other creatures and signaled them to grab us. And suddenly all the creatures started moving forward, each holding up their weapons to show us that we were in big trouble.

This has been quite a day, I thought.

I looked at Karen to see if she was going to start crying or screaming but she had this weird look on her face. She didn't look scared. She looked intense, like she was going to fight them.

"Get out the door, kid!" she yelled at me, never taking her eyes off the advancing creatures. I looked back at the little door she had shoved me through and dropped down to it. I pushed and it started to open but then quickly slammed back shut. I pushed again but something was pushing back from the outside.

"You're dead, traitors!" was all I heard through the door. It was a weird, squealy voice, like somebody had taught a pig how to talk. Whoever or whatever the voice was coming from, it was now holding the door closed.

"They're blocking the door!" I yelled to Karen as the creatures advanced on us. I had always imagined in all the action movies and science fiction films I had seen over the years that if I was ever in a dangerous situation, I'd be really cool and in control, like Indiana Jones or Luke Sky-walker or the king from *Lord of the Rings*. But the fact that my voice just sounded like a five-year-old girl's when she screams because she saw a spider made me realize that this was not about to be one of my prouder moments.

"Then grab something and help me fight these guys!" she yelled at me. And with that, she suddenly struck a pose like she thought she was in a kung fu movie, gave a war cry, and ran toward the creatures. She spun her pole over her head and then slammed it down on top of the giant octopus's fly-eye. The octopus whistled in pain, then kicked one of its spike blocks forward. Karen quickly spun and smashed her pole down on the approaching leg. This drove the spikes into the ground as the giant octopus tripped and fell forward.

Before its head even hit the floor, Karen spun the pole around her back to change hands and whipped it down on the back of its fly-eye. The octopus whistled in pain so loudly that my eardrums crackled and then it fell in a twisted, unconscious heap.

Karen spun around and swung her pole like a baseball bat, right as the huge praying mantis was charging up behind her. Her pole swung directly into the four knife-wielding arms that were about to cut her up. The force of her blow spun the bug creature sideways and Karen quickly tossed her pole in the air and grabbed it in the middle. She then started spinning the pole from side to side with both hands, like the world's deadliest baton twirler in a marching band. As the bug creature regained its balance and turned back to her, her spinning pole started knocking into all the square blades it was trying to hit her with. In a whirl of Karen's twirling staff, the blades went flying everywhere as the other creatures (and I) ducked.

One blade flew into the ceiling. Another blade stuck into the wall. Another blade flew right over my head and stuck in the little door behind me, practically giving me a haircut on its way there. Karen kept up her spinning pole attack on the mantis's loglike body; the nonstop hits sounded like some-body was playing the drums on a telephone pole.

*Crack!* She hit one of the bug creature's arms so hard that it broke off and went flying across the room, hitting the giant baby right in what I assumed was its face. (It's hard to tell when something doesn't have normal eyes.) The baby howled like a walrus and the bug screamed like an eagle, then cocked its only remaining blade back behind it in or-der to take a huge, head-cutting-off swing at Karen. Karen stopped spinning the pole and thrust it forward right into the center of the bug's body. The praying mantis stumbled back across the room and right into the giant baby, knocking them both down onto the floor with a huge *Ka-PLAM!*

Just then I heard the potato-bug thing rolling toward Karen, its one arm spinning the blade-covered wagon wheel and extending it out like a propeller to shred her into cole-slaw.

"Look out!" I yelled uselessly, since she had already seen it coming.

"Get in here and help me, kid!" she yelled as I looked around, scared out of my wits.

"How?" I yelled back.

"Grab something and start swinging!" was all she got out before she leaped in the air and just dodged the wheel of blades that the potato bug swung at her. As she was up in midair, she swung the pole down hard on top of the rolled-up creature. **_Thud!_** The pole just bounced off it as Karen fell back down onto the ground in a heap.

"Nice try!" The potato bug thing laughed in a surprisingly high voice, considering its enormous size.

It then turned and rolled forward like it was going to try to crush Karen under it but, at the last minute, Karen rolled sideways and smashed her pole right into the creature's eye.

"Eeeeeeeeeee!" the potato bug screamed as it rolled past Karen and into the wall with a thump that shook the whole room. And then it unrolled, revealing about a hundred disgusting, squirming legs all over its black underbelly. Karen then jumped up and hit a real kung fu stance as she waited for the unrolled creature to move again.

Who _is_ this girl? I wondered.

The tentacle that held the potato bug's eye turned and glared at Karen like it was really mad and then the bug curled itself back up into a ball and started rolling toward her again, its blade wheel spinning even faster than before. It started swinging the wheel back and forth so that it was like a huge swinging buzz saw. Karen looked nervous for the first time and I tried to think of what to do. I then looked over and saw a rickety-looking table lying on its side against the wall. Since my parents had just taken me to the circus a few weeks earlier and I had watched a bunch of tumblers doing lots of different stunts, I suddenly got an idea.

I grabbed the table, stood it up, and pushed it over to her. "Hey!" I yelled. "Jump on top of that guy and run!"

And with that, Karen leaped up onto the table and, right as the rolling bug swung the wheel of blades at her and cut the table in half, Karen jumped into the air and landed on top of the rolling potato bug.

The bug swung its blade wheel up at Karen but she ducked and started running on top of it, making it roll faster. They were rolling right toward the giant baby and the praying mantis creature, who were getting up groggily off the floor. The potato bug yelled in its highest voice yet, "Get out of the way!"

They looked up just in time to see Karen jump off the potato bug as it rolled right into them like a ball hitting a couple of bowling pins. They all got thrown against the wall and fell unconscious onto the ground, the potato bug unrolling itself again, its legs twitching.

"All *right!*" I yelled in victory, and that was when I got grabbed from behind.

The giant mole guy pulled me against him with his left front flipper, the large claw digging into my shoulder. He then put the sword he was holding in his right flipper against my stomach, pulling it into me so hard that if he pulled just a little more it would have cut me in half. Which is what I think he was planning to do.

"Drop your weapon or I'll turn your friend into two friends," the mole guy said to Karen as she turned to see me. She had a look on her face that showed she was less worried about my well-being than she was mad that I was there in the first place.

"Dammit!" she yelled as she saw me about to get cut in half. "I *told* you you were going to get me in trouble, kid!"

I wanted to yell "My name's Iggy, so stop calling me kid!" but, embarrassingly, I was too freaked out to say anything clever like that.

Karen kept holding the pole and the mole guy kept digging his claw harder into my shoulder and pressing his sword deeper into my stomach and I suddenly got the feeling that Karen was going to let me get killed. That was until, all of a sudden, she made an angry face and threw her pole down onto the ground as hard as she could.

The mole guy started laughing, which made him shake, which made his sword start moving back and forth across my stomach. I sucked in my gut the way my uncle Dan does whenever a pretty girl walks past him on the beach and hoped that the mole guy was going to stop finding whatever he was finding funny amusing.

"We got 'em!" he yelled loudly. And with that, a ton of uniformed creatures that sort of looked like huge three-legged armless gorillas walked in and surrounded us.

"Great work, kid," said Karen as she looked around and realized that we were completely trapped. "Way to go."

Two of the octopuses walked forward to grab Karen. She looked down at her pole but then saw how outnumbered we were and so she just sort of deflated, the way you do when you get back a test that you were sure you had earned an A on, only to find you flunked it. The octopuses were just about to grab her with their long arms when, all of a sudden . . .

. . . my cell phone rang.

# 15

# SAVED BY THE BELL. LITERALLY!

Look, *I* wasn't the one who put the goofy ring tone on my cell phone alarm. It was Ivan who thought it'd be funny to make my alarm play that song my grandpa said used to be the theme from some show called *The Lone Ranger*. The alarm always went off half an hour before my piano lesson so that I wouldn't forget to go over to Mrs. Noble's house and horrify her with how badly I played, even though I had spent the entire week practicing some song that nobody in the world would ever want to hear played on a piano, even if it was performed really well. But I always went to my lesson because my dad loved to tell me how happy I would be later in life to have a skill that could make me "the life of the party."

Well, I don't know if what happened next made me the life of the party, but I'm pretty sure it at least saved our lives.

Just as the creatures were about to grab Karen and the mole guy was about to cut me in half, I heard the *du-du-dunt/du-du-dunt/du-du-dunt-dunt-dunt* of my alarm go off. The cell phone was in my backpack, which was lying in the middle of the floor, and as soon as it went off, all the creatures stopped in their tracks as if someone had just yelled "freeze!" And the next thing I knew, as the alarm played louder and louder, the creatures all screamed and shrieked and growled and whistled and made all the other noises they made when they were scared and ran out of the room as if somebody had just rolled a live grenade into the place.

I fell onto the ground the second the mole guy let go of me, and Karen stumbled into the wall as she jumped to get out of the way of the stampeding creatures. We then looked at each other as we heard them all running and rolling and bouncing and thumping off into the distance.

"That's weird," was all I could say before Karen suddenly hopped up, grabbed me by the shirt, and started to pull me out of the room. I reached out and snagged my backpack just as Karen yanked me through the explosion hole and pulled me behind her as she ran faster than I've ever seen a girl run in my life. We sprinted through a crooked hallway with sagging ceilings and flickering lights, past uneven doorways that led to offices filled with rickety desks and all sorts

of creatures dressed in poorly fitting business suits and ties and dresses that looked like somebody had designed them in the dark. All the creatures were staring at us as we ran past, many looking terrified to see us as we raced toward the back door. Karen hit the door but it was locked. She crashed into it and then I smashed into her and we clunked our heads together like we were in a Three Stooges movie.

"OW, YOU IDIOT!" she yelled at me as she grabbed her head in pain.

"HEY, YOU'RE THE ONE WHO RAN INTO THE DOOR!" I yelled back as I grabbed *my* head in pain.

I turned and saw all the creatures looking out of their offices at us as a tall feel with lipstick on was yelling into a phone, "She's in the hallway! The Anti-Art's in the hallway!"

Karen heard this and turned back to the door.

"HELP ME BREAK THIS DOWN!" she yelled as she kicked it as hard as she could and broke it off its hinges.

"Hey, I would have helped if you'd given me a chan —" I was starting to feel sort of useless in all this as she grabbed me by the shirt again and pulled me through the doorway.

We ran away from the building and back into the curvy streets filled with the old round dwellings. I tried to keep up as Karen started pulling on my shirt so hard that it felt like it was about to rip.

"You're tearing my shirt!" I said as I stumbled along behind her.

"If you ran faster I wouldn't have to!" she yelled as we made a sharp turn and dashed between two big round buildings.

"Where are we going?" I asked, as I started to pant really hard from all the exercise I was suddenly getting. I wasn't exactly a candidate for the President's Physical Fitness Award.

"Just shut up and keep running."

And with that, we ran out from between the buildings and suddenly found ourselves flying through the air. It wasn't because Karen had magical abilities or because we had just run off the side of a cliff. It was because neither one of us saw the ten-legged creature that looked like a really long centipede with a head like a turtle. We tripped over it and slammed into the ground, then tumbled all over each other as the centipede thing looked at us and started yelling.

"Why don't you watch where you're going!" it hollered at us in a voice that sounded like a tuba. Then, suddenly, it stopped.

"ANTI-ARTS!" the thing yelled in terror as it ran off and disappeared down the curving street.

Everything was suddenly quiet as I lay on my back trying to catch my breath.

"I've got to stop for a minute," I said.

"You wanna get killed? Fine. Go ahead and rest. I'm getting out of here."

Karen tried to stand up but I was sitting on her shirttail. I heard a small rip and saw that the seam on the bottom of her shirt had just split.

"Oh, God! *Move*, kid! Haven't you done enough damage for one day?!" she said as she shoved me sideways.

Just then I heard a loud meow. We both looked over and saw the cat that thought it was a dog running toward us. It jumped through the air and landed on my chest, knocking the air out of my lungs. It then started licking my face and drooling all over me. It would have been gross if I hadn't been so happy to see the cat at that moment. Since Karen was yelling at me all the time, it was nice to find *something* that liked me.

"How can you let it do that?" Karen said as she stood and watched me get the outer layer of my face practically taken off by the cat's scratchy tongue. "I hate dogs."

"It's a cat," I said.

"Yeah, but it thinks it's a dog."

"But it looks like a cat."

"But it acts like a dog and I don't like dogs."

"Do you like cats?"

"I love cats."

"Then how can you not like something that looks like a cat?"

"Because it's not a cat. A cat's a cat because it acts like a cat. A cat's a dog if it acts like a dog."

"Yeah?" I said as I grabbed the cat and stood up. "Well, I like it because it's the only thing that's been nice to me the entire time I've been here."

"I just saved your life!" she said, sounding insulted.

"Because you had to, not because you wanted to."

"That's the most idiotic thing I've ever heard anybody say in my life! I almost died because of you and now you're mad at me because you don't like the reason I kept you from getting killed?" She glared at me, and then turned and starting walking off down the street. "Fine! Have a great time with your dog!"

"It's a *cat!*" I yelled after her. "And I will!"

I turned and looked at the empty street. Doezens of eyes were staring at me from every doorway and window. Maybe now isn't such a good time to be on my own, I thought.

"Uh . . . hey, girl?" I said nervously. "Wait up!"

And with that, I ran to catch up with Karen as the cat that thought it was a dog peed all down the front of my shirt. Again.

# 16

# A KICK IN THE NUTS

By the time Karen and I had run out of the city and were winding our way through the thickest part of another weird-looking forest, I was soaked with sweat. I had long since dropped the cat, who was now running along with us and who didn't seem to be tired at all. Actually, Karen didn't seem to be tired, either. I guess I was the only one of us who was way out of shape. "All that fast food you eat while you sit on your butt watching TV," I could hear my dad saying in my head from the frequency that now seemed so far away. It's weird how even when you're running for your life you can still feel like lying down and taking a nap. Or at least *I* could.

"Can't we stop?" I asked as well as I could with hardly any breath left in my lungs. "I think I'm gonna have a heart attack."

"Geez, kid, you're really useless, you know that?" she said over her shoulder as she kept running just as fast as ever.

"Hey, I was the one who kicked that table over to you during the fight. You would have gotten cut in half if I hadn't done that. I saved your life."

She suddenly stopped running and looked at me.

"*You* saved *my* life? If it weren't for me, you'd be dead right now!"

"Without that table, you'd be dead, too."

"No, I wouldn't."

"Yes, you would."

She stared at me for a few seconds, like she was figuring out if she should beat me up or not. I just stared at her, trying to catch my breath and figuring that if she *was* going to beat me up, I was too tired to do anything about it anyway. Finally . . .

"Thank you for pushing a table at me instead of actually picking something up and helping me fight those mutants," she said as sarcastically as she possibly could.

"Thank you for saving my life even though you've been nothing but mean to me from the second we met," I said as sarcastically as *I* possibly could.

"You're welcome," she said, just as sarcastically.

"*You're* welcome," I said, even more sarcastically.

She stared at me for another few seconds. I could only imagine what the next wave of insults was going to be. However, to my surprise . . .

"I'm Karen," she said without a smile, holding her hand out to shake mine.

I looked at her to make sure she wasn't going to flip me karate-style if I took her hand. But as near as I could tell, she seemed sincere.

I held out my hand and shook hers. "I'm Iggy."

"Gross, your hand is totally sweaty," she said, pulling her hand back and wiping it on her pants.

"Sorry," I said, feeling pretty insulted. "I've only been running for, like, five thousand miles."

"God, don't exaggerate. I know you're only, like, eleven, but try to be a bit more mature when you talk."

"Hey, I'm *twelve*," I said, even more insulted. "I'm almost thirteen, actually."

"What kind of name is Iggy?" she said, scrunching up her nose at me.

"It's short for Ignatius," I said defensively.

"Did the kids used to call you Piggy?"

"Yeah," I said, really surprised. "How did you know that?"

"Gee, that's a tough one," she said with her trademark sarcasm. "They used to call me Sarin — you know, like the poison gas — and Karen's, like, a totally normal name. So I can only imagine how bad you got it. Most of the kids in our district were total jerks."

"That's for sure."

We both nodded and then stood there, staring at each other.

For being so mean, she was sort of pretty. Really pretty, to be honest.

"What's it like being trapped here?" I finally asked her.

"It sucks," she said. "You'll see."

"Why did they try to kill us?"

"Because he knows I'll tell everybody he's a faker."

"Who?"

"*President* Arthur," she said mockingly. "What, you didn't see his name and stupid face plastered all over the place?"

"I saw that he's saying he wrote *Hamlet*."

"That's nothing. He's, like, a total fascist. He has an army and he forces everyone to like everything he does and he's completely ruining their world. He's totally out of his mind."

"I know who he is," I said, trying to impress her. "He used to be a teacher at my school."

"No duh, dimwit," she said, raising her eyebrow at me. "He used to be *my* teacher. And now he's freaking out because he knows I can totally bust him."

"How does he know you're here?"

She gave me a look that showed she was trying to fig-ure out whether she was going to tell me the story or not. Then . . .

"Because when I first got here, I went to him for help. I didn't know where I was and when I saw his picture I was really happy, because I liked him in junior high and thought for sure he'd be able to fix everything. I went to the stupid mansion he lives in and he was really excited to see me. He told me all about how he got here and about the frequencies and how much he hated it back home and for a while it was lots of fun.

"But then I started seeing all the stuff he was doing, how he was trying to pass off everything from our frequency as stuff he came up with, and how he was acting like he was some kind of god or something. He was forcing everybody living here to speak English and to dress like we do and making them build all his buildings and having his army beat them and throw them in jail or worse if they didn't do whatever he said. And so I started giving him a hard time about it, telling him to stop acting like such a dictator and trying to tell all the creatures in this world who he really is and what he's doing. And the next thing I knew, some of his guards came and locked me in his basement and told me I couldn't leave. Like, ever."

"So you escaped?" I asked, feeling sort of sick to my stomach that Mr. Arthur turned out to be such a mean guy.

"Yeah. When he came to see me and tell me that he couldn't let me ruin things by telling everybody what was up, I jumped on him and got him in a headlock and told his guards that I was going to break his neck unless they let me go. Fortunately, he's such a wuss that I was totally stronger than him, and he was completely freaked out that I might

hurt him. So he told all the guards to back off and I kept him in a headlock and dragged him all the way to the front gates. And once they opened them to let me out, I kicked him in the nuts and ran away. His guards have been after me ever since."

"So did you tell everybody that he's a fake?"

"I tried, but he told the whole town that I was trying to kill him and that I was this evil spirit from another world and he put my picture all over the place and since everybody here has to believe everything that he tells them, they all just scream and run away when they see me and then they tell his army where I am and his goons come after me and try to kill me." Then she sighed and shook her head. "To be honest, it's getting pretty old."

She looked around like she was figuring out where to run next but I could tell that she was actually trying not to show me how depressed she was about how her life was going at that moment. It was the first time I had seen her actually act like a normal person and not some mean girl or kung fu master or drill sergeant. And I sorta felt sorry for her.

"Then why did you come back to town?" I asked.

She gave me a look like she couldn't understand why I would ask her something so stupid and said as casually as you would if you were telling somebody you were about to go to the grocery store . . .

"Because I'm trying to figure out how to get the town to turn against him."

I stared at her for a few seconds, then I took off my backpack, opened it, and pulled out my dad's Shakespeare book. I held it up to her and, with my next six words, tried to sound as cool as I possibly could.

"Do you think this might help?"

**17**

## PUH PAH

As Karen and I ran through the woods — well, actually, I sort of stumbled along as she ran, pulling me by my shirt-sleeve — I had never seen her look so happy. Granted, I hadn't known her that long and "I had never seen her look so happy" is usually a sentence you say when somebody you've known for years who never smiles finally smiles. But it was still true. I mean, I hadn't seen her happy at all in the short amount of time I had known her.

When I showed Karen the Shakespeare book, her eyes lit up the way they might have if I had given her a diamond ring or something else that girls go all nutty over. Then she grabbed it from me, flipped through it to make sure I hadn't just handed her a phone book with a Shakespeare cover glued onto it, and said, "Now they're really going to believe me!" And then she grabbed my shirtsleeve and that's how we got where we currently were, which was running through the woods.

She darted in and out of all the odd-looking trees that were fortunately much farther apart than they had been around the dead field. All the strange colors of the different plants and leaves in the forest sort of made it feel like we were running through the woods during the fall. But the extra purples and blues and other colors that didn't really look like anything I had ever seen before made it seem like somebody had melted a box of crayons and poured it all over the forest.

"Where . . . are we . . . going?" I asked as I tried to catch my breath, which isn't easy when you're running at top speed.

"We've gotta show this to Herfta," she yelled over her shoulder to me. "And don't ask me who that is. You'll see in a minute."

"I wasn't . . . going . . . to ask you."

"Sure you were. It's only normal to ask who someone is when somebody tells you that person's name but then doesn't tell you anything else about them."

"Then why'd you tell me not to ask?"

"Hey, just because it's normal for you to ask doesn't mean I want to answer. If we get into a situation where just because you've arrived in a completely different world that

I've been in for a year you feel it's okay to start asking me '*What's* that?' and '*Who's* that?' and '*Why* is that like *that?*' every five seconds, then I'm going to end up wanting to kill you after about three minutes. And since I'm going to need your help now, I think it'd be better if we do everything we can to make sure you don't drive me crazy."

"Wait a minute," I said. "What if you drive *me* crazy?"

"Then you can feel free to keep your mouth shut about it."

"Hey, that's not fair."

"Tough. I was here first." She looked back at me and I thought I almost saw something close to what some people might call a "playful smile" on her face. For two seconds, I started to wonder if she was deciding that she might actually not completely hate having me around. That was, until she yanked on my shirt and said, "God, would you run already? You're slower than my grandma."

And so, not wanting to be slower than anybody's grandmother, I did my best to try to speed up.

\*     \*     \*

After what felt like half an hour, I was ready to die. We had been running nonstop, and I was sweating like a pig. The cat raced along next to us the whole time, and Karen didn't seem tired at all. I had to wonder if living in a strange world surrounded by bizarre creatures and getting chased by strange armies that want to kill you would make anybody into a person or cat who could run for half an hour and not get tired. Karen didn't even look like she was sweating.

Karen suddenly stopped running and since I was so deep in thought about gross stuff like her sweat glands, I basically plowed right into her, knocking her down and knocking the Shakespeare book out of her hand.

"Don't you ever watch where you're going, kid?" she yelled at me as she jumped back up and grabbed the book off the ground.

My body was so happy to have stopped running that suddenly my legs turned into Jell-O and I collapsed onto the ground in front of her, panting like I had just . . . uh . . . well, like I had just run for a freakin' half an hour straight. "I . . . think . . . I'm going to . . . die," I said, unable to catch my breath as the cat jumped onto my chest and stared at me.

"All right, drama queen," she said with a shake of her head. "We're here anyway."

And that was when I opened my eyes and looked up at the sky.

Yikes.

We were in the middle of a dense patch of those trees that had the spikes and thorns all over them. But these trees were really tall. I mean, like, skyscraper tall. And way up at the top of the trees was an entire city of tree houses. Except they were way more elaborate than regular tree houses. There were round ones and oval ones and huge ones and tiny ones and yet none of them had any kind of bridge or walkway between them. It looked like whoever lived up there had to jump from one house to the next, which seemed insane because it looked pretty impossible to jump that far and, even if you could, chances were you'd eventually miss and fall hundreds of feet to your death. What a weird place, I thought as I moved the cat off my chest and stood up to get a better look.

And that was when I noticed something.

At first it just looked like a lot of birds were flying around the treetops. But then I quickly realized that what I was seeing was a bunch of people with wings, just like the girl I had seen when I first woke up in the dead field, and they were flying around from house to house and building to building, hundreds of them. As I watched them fly, I saw that their treetop city looked like it went on forever in all directions, with some buildings so big that they covered the tops of four or five trees and blocked all the sunlight from getting down to where Karen and I were.

*WWWWWWWHHHHEEEEEETTTTTT!* Karen whistled super loud and I almost had a heart attack because she did it right behind my head. I'd tried my whole life to be able to do one of those loud whistles — you know, the kind where you put your fingers in your mouth and blow really hard (some people can do it without even using their fingers, although they have to do this weird curly thing with their tongue against their teeth and their lips all pursed like they just ate a lemon or something) — but had never been able to do it.

"God, warn me when you do that!" I said, my heart now racing even faster than it had been from running.

"Toughen up, you wuss," she said as she squinted up at the treetops. I saw the cat look up. Suddenly its eyes filled with fear. I threw my head back and saw a bunch of flying people coming down toward us. They were flying so fast I was sure they were going to zoom right past us and smash into the ground like pennies tossed off the Empire State Building. The cat took off running as fast as it could and disappeared into the woods as I stood sort of paralyzed. As the flying people sped toward us, I could see that they were as strange looking as the girl I saw over the dead field. Their arms and legs seemed to be extraordinarily long and their bodies were pretty skinny, which I guess makes sense. I mean, it'd be pretty hard to fly if you were fat. My cousin Ernie had a parrot that was really fat and all it did was sit in its cage all day and say "super-duper party pooper" over and over again until you wanted to strangle it.

When they were almost on top of me, I screamed and ducked down as if that would do any good if a flying guy landed on top of me. **Whoosh!** A blast of air hit me, and leaves and dirt blew up all around as the flying people used their wings to stop themselves. Then their feet softly touched the ground, as if they hadn't just been zooming toward the earth at a billion miles per hour.

"*Poo pa-poo pah fuh puh*," I heard a voice say. But the voice didn't really "say" any of it. It sounded more like a really quiet person was trying to blow a piece of fuzz out from between his lips.

I looked up to see that the voice was coming from the tallest person I'd ever seen. Everything about him was stretched, as if he were made out of wax and somebody had heated him up and then grabbed his head and feet and pulled to make him longer, like a big piece of taffy. He was standing with a bunch of other flying people, both men and women, who looked a lot like he did, only not as crazy tall.

"*Pah poo fuh puh hoo poo*," said Karen back to the super tall guy. But she said it almost the same way that he had said it, all soft and breathy, which impressed me because it didn't sound anything like her normal, occasionally obnoxious voice. She said it really fast and excited, which made her kind of sound like a cat having a sneezing fit. Then she held up the Shakespeare book to him and said another bunch of *pah*s and *puh*s, and pointed at me.

The super tall guy walked over and looked me up and down, then looked back at Karen like he was surprised that another person from our frequency was now in his world.

He exchanged a look with his flying buddies and then turned back and held out his hand to me.

"Hello," he said in a really soft and quiet voice. "My name is Herfta."

As surprised as I was to hear him speak English, I tried to act cool and so grabbed his hand to give it a good firm shake, the way my dad always said you should shake somebody's hand. "Nobody likes shaking hands with a wet noodle," he used to say. He obviously hadn't shaken hands with Herfta. "Hi, I'm Ig —"

**CRUNCH!**

"YEOUWWW!!!" Herfta screamed in a loud, high-pitched voice that almost sounded like a cat getting its tail stepped on. Herfta's hand was about as strong as a piece of Kleenex and it snapped in my hand like a sheet of balsa wood.

"IGGY!" yelled Karen as Herfta jumped around, shaking his hand and putting it between his knees the way you do when you hit your thumb with a hammer, while the other flying people swarmed around him to make sure he was all right. "WHY'D YOU DO THAT?"

"Do *what?!*" I shrieked back, completely freaked out that I had just broken the hand of some being from another frequency. "I shook his hand like he wanted me to! What was I supposed to do?!"

"They don't shake hands here!" she yelled as if I was the biggest moron to ever walk the planet. "You were just supposed to press your palm up against his."

"HOW WAS I SUPPOSED TO KNOW THAT?!" I said, my voice cracking.

"You didn't give me a chance to tell you!" she said as she went over to Herfta and inspected his wounded hand.

"You had, like, a whole half hour while we were running!" I yelled. "You couldn't have said, 'Hey, I'm going to introduce you to some flying people in a few minutes and when I do, make sure you don't shake their hands because you'll crush them like a bunch of twigs'?"

Herfta looked at me as the other flying people tried to repair his hand. His voice sounded like he was still in a lot of pain. "I'm assuming that . . . what you did . . . isn't an act of aggression . . . where you're from," he said, sounding a bit like a constipated guy sitting on the toilet trying to take a poo.

"Um, no, sir," I said, still surprised that he spoke English so well. "It's something nice you do when you first meet someone. Didn't Karen ever shake hands with anybody here?"

"No," she said in a majorly sarcastic way. "I, unlike you, don't just assume because we do something in our world that everybody else in the universe does the same thing."

"I was trying to be nice!"

"Yeah," she said, her eyes looking at Herfta's smashed hand and then back at me. "Great work."

Man, there were so many times when I wanted to put a spider down the back of her shirt. Except in this frequency it was probably some kind of compliment or something.

Karen and Herfta *puh*ed and *pah*ed for a little while longer, then Herfta gestured to another flying guy and motioned up at the treetops with his hurt hand and suddenly a huge wooden bowl-type thing dropped down out of the trees and thumped loudly onto the ground behind me, making me jump. There was a rope attached to it that was used to lift it up and down to the treetops.

"Okay, hand crusher," Karen said, motioning her head toward the wooden bowl. "Get in. They said they'll let you into their city, even though you just wounded their leader."

"But I didn't . . . I . . ." I tried to defend myself again but realized it was just a big waste of breath. I simply sighed the way you do when your mom accuses you of eating something that the dog actually ate, and then climbed into the wooden bowl with Karen.

I looked to see if the cat was around so I could bring it with me but the second we were in the bowl, we were pulled up into the air so fast that I thought I was either going to barf or my pants were going to fall down from the G-force. I looked and saw Herfta and his flying companions speeding next to our wooden elevator, flying straight up into the air, hardly even moving their wings. A couple of the flying people gave me sort of dirty looks as we were zooming up toward the treetops but I was too freaked out to really do anything about it. I guess they had the right to be mad at me since I did crush their leader's hand, even though it was his fault for holding it out to me without letting me know that he was made out of the equivalent of pipe cleaners and fragile glassware and other super breakable stuff.

*SSSSS–WUMP!* As fast as we took off, we stopped even faster. I guess they were used to people stopping that fast because I flew up and hit my head against a really soft padded piece of something that didn't hurt. I'd hate to have been the person who made them first realize that super-fast-bowl-flying-up-at-top-speed plus extremely-sudden-stop equals person-in-wooden-bowl-smashing-his-or-her-head. Because without that padded thing my head would have felt a lot like Herfta's hand did at that moment.

I looked down from the padded thingamajig and stared out in front of me. Stretched out before me was an entire city built onto the tops of the trees. From the ground I had thought that the tree houses were going to be sort of like tree houses were back home, all rickety and small, like the one Gary's dad built for him in their backyard. That tree house was so junky that once when we were trying to have a sleepover in it, the floor broke and Ivan — who had made us zip him all the way up in his "cocoon" bag so that only his face was showing — fell through and ended up draped over a big branch looking like a huge worm that somebody had dropped on a stick.

The tree buildings up here were like real buildings, except that they were really tall and crazy-looking. Every building had a roof that came to some kind of point at the top, sort of like steeples on churches, except that these points were really thin and tall, like huge skinny ice-cream cones or knitting needles.

There were tons of different heights and sizes of buildings and they seemed to go on for half a mile. They all had openings with little perches and gangplanks sticking out like tiny landing strips that the flying people were using to come in and out of the buildings like bees going in and out of hives. And all the buildings were decorated with sticks and branches that had been twisted and woven into big curvy shapes that looked like the edges of these lace placemat thingies my grandma had all over her house. Grandma called them *doilies* but that just seems like the kind of word that can get a twelve-year-old boy beaten up if he even thinks about saying it.

Karen caused all kinds of commotion once we were up there, *puh*ing and *pah*ing and passing around my Shakespeare book to some other flying people, both men and women, who were almost as tall as Herfta. They would occasionally speak in English when it seemed like Karen didn't know how to say something in flying-people language. It became clear pretty fast that these tall ones were the leaders of the treetop city. After Karen stopped talking to them, they all went off to discuss whatever she had told them about me and my Shakespeare book.

"What's up?" I said as I walked up next to her.

"I'm trying to convince them to do something about Mr. Arthur," she said, sounding a bit impatient. "The Puhluvians are really cool people but they sort of don't care about anything that happens on the ground. They're kind of snobby that way. It comes from living in treetops for so long."

"How'd you learn to speak their language?"

"They taught me." She shrugged as if I should have been able to figure that out without asking.

"But they speak English. You didn't have to learn their language."

"Yeah, and I didn't have to save you, either, but I did," she said, sounding like she was once again getting upset with me. "It's called being interested in things and wanting to expand my horizons. Try it sometime."

Before I could make some sarcastic comment that I hadn't yet thought of at that moment, I suddenly got the weird feeling that somebody was watching me. I don't know how I could tell that somebody's eyes were focused on me because it wasn't like they were touching me or standing where I could see them. It was just more like a hunch, like when you suddenly get a feeling that the phone might ring and then it does.

I turned and saw a face looking at me from behind one of the twisty stick decorations. And I immediately knew who it was.

It was the flying girl I saw when I first arrived.

The second she saw me look at her she pulled her face back out of sight. I was going to follow her but right then Herfta and the tall people came back up to Karen.

"*Fwuh puh*," Herfta said to Karen, with a nod.

"Excellent," said Karen, giving me a nod.

I nodded back, having no idea what I was nodding about, as I heard a bunch of loud horns blast out all over the tree-top city.

Something was about to happen.

# 18

## "IDIOTS!"

I was in a football stadium once when my dad took Gary and Ivan and me to see a monster truck rally. None of us were really into monster trucks but for some reason my dad thought it would be a fun thing to do. It wasn't bad, either, until this giant drag-racing tractor spun its huge tires in some mud down at our end of the stadium and sprayed us with tons of oily sludge that smelled like gasoline. We had to leave soon after that because Ivan started to feel sick and we all knew he could throw up at the drop of a hat. (He threw up at our house once when my mom put a piece of pecan pie with a hair on it in front of him, even though it was her hair and she washed her hair every day. Ivan never ate at our house again after that.)

The reason I bring up that football stadium is because when we followed Herfta and the other city leaders to the far edge of the tree building and rounded the corner and stepped out onto a big ornate platform that overlooked the rest of the treetop city, there was suddenly a huge football stadium filled with flying people, thousands of them, stretched out before us. Only there was no stadium. The flying people were hovering midair in the shape of a huge oval arena, like someone had pulled the stadium out from under them but left them floating in place. It was a pretty amazing sight and since they were all in perfect formation around the official-looking platform we were standing on, I had to assume this was what they did whenever Herfta and the other leaders wanted to talk to them.

Herfta stepped out to the front of the platform and raised his hands in the air and suddenly the entire floating stadium of flying people starting going *fup fup fup* in unison. They all did it in that super quiet breathy way that I was discovering flying people always talked in, but when thousands of people do it all at the same time, it's amazing how loud it can get.

Herfta kept his arms up in the air and turned slowly back and forth so that every side of the stadium could see him and I started to feel like he was milking it way too long. He even used his hands to sort of signal people to keep chanting for him. Yes, this included the hand that he made such a big deal out of me hurting, which now seemed to be causing him no pain at all as he used to wave for them to keep *fup*ing at him.

Finally, he put his palms out to make them stop and then he started *puh*ing and *pah*ing in a really quiet voice. I had to figure that flying people have super powerful ears because nobody yelled "Speak up!" or even looked like they were having a hard time hearing him. They just flapped their wings silently and listened to Herfta, who went on for about five minutes.

As he talked, he kept pointing at Karen and then at me and then finally he pointed at the Shakespeare book that Karen was holding. At one point, I saw all the flying people suddenly look at each other and make faces that seemed to indicate they were thinking *Huh, that's interesting* about whatever Herfta had just said. Then, Herfta finally turned to Karen and signaled for her to come up to the front of the platform.

Karen stepped up and I suddenly got this really nervous feeling in my stomach, as if it were me stepping up to talk to the stadium of people. I had never liked having to give presentations or read out loud in front of the class or even do show-and-tell when I was little. To see all the faces of my classmates who didn't really like me staring and waiting for me to say something that they had already decided wouldn't be interesting was sort of more than my fragile ego could take. I preferred to just stay in my seat and act like I wasn't really even in the room in those situations, since whenever my classmates *did* notice me they tended to be mean to me. And so seeing Karen about to talk to so many thousands of people just made me want to throw up.

As you can tell, I've got "issues," as the school psychiatrist calls them.

Karen held up the Shakespeare book and started talking in the puh-pah language. She really spoke well and I was pretty in awe of her for being so good at it. Whenever I hear somebody who normally speaks English speaking a foreign language I get majorly impressed. Like, I have a cousin who is really good at French — so good that she has a French boyfriend who barely speaks English — and whenever I heard her talking to him I felt like she was a genius or something.

I took a beginning Spanish class last semester and after four months all I could say was "Hello" and "Where's the library?" and one day when we ate at a Mexican restaurant I asked the waiter where the library was and he started laughing really hard and told my mom that I had just said something super dirty. So Karen was impressing the heck out of me, since this flying-people language was about as weird as it gets.

She went on for about fifteen minutes and was pretty passionate about what she was saying. She later told me she was letting them know all about how I had come to this frequency the same way she and Mr. Arthur had, and that the book I had brought with me proved Mr. Arthur had passed off *Hamlet* and all the other stuff he said he wrote as his own when in fact he was simply stealing the best ideas and creative stuff that had been done in our world by other people. She said it was up to them to help her rebel against Mr. Arthur and rally all the other creatures in Lesterville to rise up against him and free themselves from his egomaniacal tyranny, or something like that.

She made the case that to allow Mr. Arthur to continue getting away with what he was doing was like helping him destroy the cultures of all the ground-dwelling creatures who had lived their lives just fine before Mr. Arthur started forcing them all to speak English and do all the things he thought they should do. The future of their frequency was at stake, even though Mr. Arthur seemed to be leaving the flying people alone at this point. It was only a matter of time before he figured out a way to change their culture and oppress them, too, she said. And so he must be stopped.

She ended her speech *puh*ing and *pah*ing so forcefully that spit was flying out of her mouth. One of the drawbacks of flying-people language seemed to be that it wasn't a very good language to yell in, which made it about the worst language for a hothead like Karen to communicate in. It made me wish I only spoke Puhluvian so that she couldn't yell at me as much. But, as she was proving right then, she had figured out a way to raise her voice in another species' language, too. Well done, Karen.

She stared at all the flying people for what felt like a really long time and then turned and walked back to me. "If that doesn't wake them up, nothing will," she whispered as she turned back to the crowd and watched as Herfta went up in front of them again.

Herfta raised his hand and asked them a question, as if he were asking them to vote on what Karen had said. She gave me a nervous look that said she was hoping for something good to happen. When Herfta finished his question, all the flying people looked around at each other, as if they were considering what to do. They didn't nod or shake their heads or anything that showed what they were thinking. They did this for about two minutes and the way Karen was fidgeting around and clearing her throat and rubbing her nose nervously I could tell she was about to lose her mind from the suspense of it all.

Then, finally, all the flying people stopped looking at each other and turned back to Herfta. He scanned his eyes over everybody in the stadium, then put his arms straight out to the sides and lifted his palms skyward as if to say, "Well?"

Karen held her breath. I stared at all the flying people. Their faces didn't give me any indication of what they were thinking. And then, suddenly . . .

"*CHUP!*"

The whole stadium said it loud and at the same time. It was the loudest thing I'd heard from them before or since.

I looked at Karen. She shook her head, mad.

"Idiots!" she said to herself, then shoved the Shakespeare book into my hands and stormed off the platform. Actually, she said a word before "idiots" that I don't think I should write here because my dad always said that swearing is the sign of a small mind and that if you started using bad words, you'd no longer be able to communicate without them. But please realize that just because I censored Karen's statement I'm not saying that Karen has a small mind. Because she doesn't. And, man, she'd really beat me up if she thought I said that.

I turned to watch Karen go and saw the flying girl peeking around the corner at me again. She once again pulled her head back behind the wall the second she saw me. But only after I saw that she was smiling at me. And, man, was she pretty when she smiled.

"C'mon!" Karen snapped at me over her shoulder as she headed off around the opposite corner.

"I'm coming," I said as I stuffed the Shakespeare book into my backpack and ran off to catch up with her, not at all sure why I had been doing everything she told me to do ever since we met.

# 19

## FOO

Karen wasn't much fun to be in a small room with.

But there we were, together in a small room.

The flying people had given her an apartment to live in when she met them a year ago and the two of us were sitting in there as Karen stewed about the huge "*chup*" she had gotten a half hour earlier. When I say "apartment," I mean a tiny room built out of lots of sticks and twigs that had been woven into a super strong sort of wicker. It was the same type of material that my grandma's ancient lawn furniture was made out of, except her chairs were all white and faded and covered with bird doodies and were so old that whenever you sat in them, they creaked and bent like they were about to disintegrate into a pile of dust. Once I got up from one of them really fast and a piece of broken wicker got hooked on the back of my shorts and tore open a huge hole on the one day I wasn't wearing underwear because my mom forgot to do the laundry. So everyone at our family reunion saw my butt crack when I turned around to look at the chair, and my cousin Philip called me Rear Window for the next year.

The floor in Karen's apartment was stronger than my grandma's chairs but it still creaked and bent when I walked over it. Karen said that the flying people had made her floors stronger than they usually did for themselves because she weighed so much more than them since they have super light bones. As I got up and walked over to look at some weird mural hanging on her wall, the floor creaked so loudly that I got nervous it might break. So did Karen, apparently.

"This apartment's only made for one person, you know," she said to me testily. "So could you at least stop walking around and just sit on the opposite side of the room so that the weight is evenly distributed?"

That was easy for her to say. She was sitting on her super soft bed that looked like it was stuffed with feathers and fluff. All I had to sit in was a chair on the opposite side of the room that had been made out of three thick branches and was about as comfortable as sitting on a pile of firewood. But since she was in such a bad mood, I figured I should just sit down and not antagonize her.

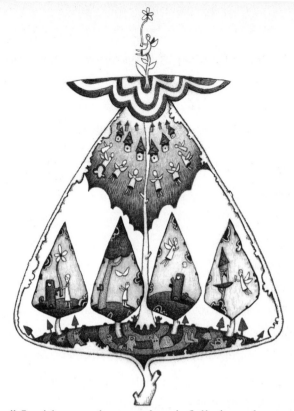

"So," I said as my butt sank painfully into the super uncomfortable chair, "why did they say no?"

"Because they just don't care," she said with a shake of her head. "They've always lived up in the treetops and since they're the only things in this world that can fly, they've never had to deal with anything on the ground. Their food all comes from the tops of trees, they build their cities out of materials from the tops of trees, and their bodies are so fragile they could really only get hurt by ground creatures.

"And so they want nothing to do with anything down there and as far as the Mr. Arthur thing goes, they all just think the ground creatures are stupid anyway and so they deserve what they get. Herfta says if someone like Arthur can convince them to do everything he says even though there's only one of him and thousands and thousands of them, then it's their fault for being so easily manipulated."

"He's sort of right, isn't he?" I said, feeling pretty certain Karen would yell at me for saying that. But she didn't.

"I guess so." She sighed. "But it doesn't mean the flying people shouldn't do something to help. Just being smarter than the ground creatures should make them want to stop anybody from taking advantage of them. Especially when I just proved to them that Arthur's been passing off other people's accomplishments as his own. I really thought that would drive them crazy, since they respect art and intellect and fairness. But it seems they only care about those things if they exist in their treetop world. It's really depressing."

She fell back on her bed and sighed again.

"So . . ." I said uncertainly, "what do we do now?"

"I don't know." She shrugged. I couldn't *see* her shrug because she was lying down but the way she said "I don't know" sure sounded like she had just done a major-league shrug with her shoulders.

"This really sucks," Karen said. "If we hang out on the ground we get chased by Arthur's army and if we stay up here there's no way we can do anything to stop him. And we can't even really do anything up here because most of the city isn't reinforced for us to walk on and we can't get from building to building because we can't fly."

I was going to suggest that we just get back to the ground and take our chances but then I remembered how close we had come to getting killed when Arthur's soldiers had caught us. I had to imagine that my cell phone alarm ringing could only save us so many times before they figured out what it was or stopped being scared of it. I pulled out the phone and looked at it and saw that we didn't even have that line of defense anymore: the battery was about to die because I forgot to turn it off. Good going, Iggy.

Karen was now quiet and lost in thought. Since I didn't know what to say and my butt was practically numb from the branches in the chair cutting off my circulation, I stood up and walked out of the room. Karen could clearly hear the floor creaking as I left but she didn't even bother to say anything. It was the first time I'd seen her actually quiet. Sadly, I didn't enjoy it as much as I thought I would.

I went to the wooden railing at the edge of the walkway outside Karen's room. I looked over the side and couldn't get over how high up we were. I've never been afraid of heights, but my mom is. She freaks out if we get a room on the second floor of a motel, so I could only imagine what kind of meltdown she would have if she was standing on a rather rickety walkway suspended a few hundred feet off the ground. But I liked the feeling of being this high up.

I could understand why the flying people sort of didn't care what was going on below them. If I could fly in my frequency, I can guarantee I would do everything possible to not interact with the people who were mean to me on the ground. I guess I'd still hang out with Gary and Ivan and my mom and dad but since they wouldn't be able to fly, I could see even getting bored with them. And so if there were other people who could fly, I'd probably spend more time with them and less time with my earthbound friends and family. Well, unless the other flying people were jerks. I mean, if the only other people who could fly were Frank Gutenkunitz and his bully friends then that would be about as bad as it could get, unless the fact that we all were able to fly suddenly made them decide we had a lot in common and should agree to see the best in each other. But then I couldn't imagine what would be the best inside Frank and his goons, even if they *could* fly. They'd still be the mean bullies who made my life miserable but now they'd be able to chase me through the sky and beat me up in the tops of trees in addition to making my life terrible on the ground.

Man, I couldn't even have a good daydream about the world I had left that morning. Maybe it was better that I *was* trapped in this frequency.

Before I could think about that for too long, I noticed that the cat who thought it was a dog was down at the bottom of the tree with its paws on the trunk and its tail wagging, staring up at me. The cat was too far away for me to yell down to and since I didn't want to disturb anybody, I just waved at it. Apparently the cat had really good eyesight because it spun around in a circle like it was excited and I heard the faintest meow come from it. Man, this cat was loyal, if nothing else.

As I stared down at it, I felt someone else looking at me. I turned and saw the girl again. But this time, she didn't disappear. She looked a bit startled at first, but then she just stood there and stared at me. The setting sun was making everything turn orangey brown, and her white clothes and pale skin made her almost appear to be glowing. She was sort of dressed the way kids are when they play angels in school recitals, except her outfit was prettier than that. It was like a long nightgown or robe but it had lots of twirly patterns embroidered on it. She had a belt tied around her waist that showed how thin she was, and on her feet she was wearing white shoes that sort of looked like ballet slippers except that they were pointier and had almost foamy-looking soles. And she was really really pretty. Like, she'd be the prettiest girl in my school hands down and Cheryl Biggs would probably go insane trying to get her transferred so that the flying girl wouldn't be more popular than she was.

I just stared at her, probably looking like an idiot, before I finally summoned up the courage to say something.

"Hi," I said like somebody who had just been hit in the head really hard. Then I immediately realized she probably didn't even know what "hi" meant.

"Hi," she said back in her super soft flying-people voice. And, just like you'd expect from somebody who's really pretty, she had a really pretty voice, too. It was sweet and friendly and sounded lighter than air. "I'm Foo."

I was sort of shocked that she spoke English, although I guess I shouldn't have been since I'd heard Herfta speak it, too. "Hi. I'm Iggy," I said in a quiet voice, the way I'd talk if my lazy uncle Mel was sleeping on the couch like he did every time he ate lunch at our house.

"Iggy?" she said with a smile, like she was trying not to laugh at my name. "What does that mean?"

"Uh . . ." I didn't expect that question. I didn't really expect any question, since just seconds before I didn't even think she could speak my language. "I don't know, really. I don't think it means anything. If it does, it's probably something embarrassing. What does Foo mean?"

She pointed up with her finger. "Raindrop," she said, sounding a bit embarrassed. "My dad said I fell from the sky. I don't really know what that means but he always smiles when he says it."

"Huh, that's weird," I said, unsure if I should laugh or not. But I didn't laugh since I didn't want to insult her because she was the prettiest girl who ever talked to me without calling me Piggy or saying "Get out of the way, weirdo," or "This is the *girls'* bathroom, you moron."

"Are you really from that other world, too?" she said with a look on her face that showed she'd be really impressed if I said yes. So, you can imagine what I said next.

"Yes."

Man, am I smooth.

She smiled and walked forward a few steps. "Is it true that nobody can fly there?"

"Yeah, pretty much. I mean, birds can fly but they're animals and they can't talk or do anything other than fly, really. And people can sort of fly but only if they're in these big things called airplanes that are made out of metal and use a lot of gas to get off the ground. They're really loud, lose your luggage sometimes, and used to give you free food but now make you pay, like, five dollars for a box with a Fig Newton and some raisins in it. But I think we all sort of wish we *could* fly like you guys do. Or, I mean, I wish *I* could, anyway."

She stared at me and I immediately felt like I had just made a fool out of myself. But after a few seconds, she smiled and gave a little laugh.

"You're funny," she said softly.

And then I sort of felt like I was going to have a heart attack.

But a really good heart attack.

## MORE FOO

My stomach knotted up like somebody grabbed it and twisted it sideways, and my chest felt like it had gotten hit really hard with a hammer. I'm pretty sure my eyes went wide when she said I was funny and I was worried that her smile was going to turn into the universal girl eyebrow-fur-row-and-frown that says "What's your problem?" But she just kept smiling at me.

Does she like me? I wondered, embarrassed that I could even consider that someone who looked like her could like someone who looked like me.

"So," I said, now suddenly really nervous, "what's it like living here?" Oh, man, what a stupid question.

"It's nice, I guess. I've never lived anywhere else. Do you like it?"

"Yeah, it's really cool. I mean, I've only been up here less than an hour, I think. But it's really pretty and it's nice being up this high." Then, for some reason, the next question popped into my head, which I immediately blurted out: "Was that you flying over the field when I first got here?"

"Yeah," she said, looking embarrassed. "I'm sorry. I know I shouldn't spy on people. But I was just flying back from the water place and looked down and suddenly there you were. Since the only other people like you I'd ever seen were Karen and Mr. Arthur, I couldn't help but stare."

"You've seen Mr. Arthur?" I asked, a bit surprised for some reason that a flying person would have seen him.

"Yes, but don't tell anybody. We're all forbidden to fly over the city ever since Mr. Arthur took over."

"Why?"

"Because nobody wants him to think about us. They figure that if he doesn't see us he'll just leave us alone."

"That makes sense, I guess. But how come you still do it?"

She looked down, like she was feeling guilty, and I suddenly wanted to kick myself for asking her the kind of question someone's father might ask. But before I could apologize . . .

"Because I sort of like what he's doing. I think all those things he's building are interesting and I like the way they look. And I like to hear that music he makes. It's pretty."

I've always had a hard time disagreeing with people I like and it was even harder at that moment to disagree with a beautiful girl who I thought was maybe starting to like me. But I sort of felt like I had to say something.

"Well, I guess it's pretty if you've never heard it before, but if you heard the music it was based on back in my world, you'd think his version of it is sort of terrible." It came out meaner than I wanted it to but I guess I was starting to feel as mad at Mr. Arthur as Karen was.

"But if I hear it and think it's pretty, doesn't that mean it's still good?" She didn't ask it in a sarcastic way, the way Karen would say something like that. She was asking a sincere question. And it kinda stumped me.

"Well . . . I guess," I said weakly because it just didn't seem like the right answer. "But if you heard the real version of the song and the voice of the guy who really sang it in my world, then the next time you heard Mr. Arthur's version you'd say, 'Man, that's terrible.'"

"But since I can't hear that version, then isn't it okay for me to like what Mr. Arthur did?" she asked as innocently as if she were asking me why the sky was blue. "And doesn't the fact that you are so used to your version that you can't hear what's good about his version mean that the version you like is keeping you from enjoying something that you might like if you didn't know how it was really supposed to sound?"

"Uh . . ." I said, sounding once again like a guy who just got hit in the head. Man, for somebody who just learned how to speak English she could sure talk circles around me, the guy who has been speaking the language his whole life. "I guess so."

She studied my face for a few seconds, then said, "Do you miss your world?"

"I . . . uh . . . I don't know. I mean, I hate the thought that my parents and my friends might think I'm dead, but it was sort of a place that I never felt very comfortable in."

"I don't feel very comfortable here, either," she said quietly. "Everybody spends so much time saying bad things about the Chuparians and being so judgmental about each other that I just feel like flying away for good sometimes."

"The Chuparians?" I asked, confused.

She looked a bit embarrassed. "That's what they call everyone who lives on the ground. I feel bad even saying the word. It's not a very nice term. Or at least it gets used in pretty mean ways up here."

"Huh," I said as a cool breeze lightly blew Foo's hair. "I guess it's kinda like how everybody where I live hates the people in the town next to ours because our high school football team loses to their team all the time. It's so bad that you can't even be friends with anybody from that town. My friend's older sister dated a guy from there once and the whole school stopped talking to her. Just because of stupid football games."

She thought about this for a second, then said, "My father would be very upset if he knew I liked Lesterville. He'd probably lock me in my room forever."

"Yeah, my dad gets pretty overdramatic about stuff, too. Fortunately, he thinks the whole football rivalry thing is dumb," I said, suddenly starting to miss him. "He does a lot of embarrassing things but he's a pretty good guy."

"I love my dad, too, but he doesn't take anything I say seriously." She gave a little sigh and looked out at the tree-top city. "I never stand up to him or anybody here because it's just not worth it. They'll never change their minds."

"Yeah, neither will the people in my town."

We looked at each other, realizing we were both sort of in the same boat in our two different worlds. The only difference was I wasn't sure if I would ever see *my* world again.

She suddenly smiled and stepped close to me. "Can I touch your face?"

A second heart attack hit me. This time it was like somebody had just driven a truck into my chest. I can pretty much guarantee that I didn't hide my surprise at her request, mainly because she suddenly stopped and looked embarrassed.

"I'm sorry," she said like a little kid who had just broken something. "I need to go."

And with that, she turned and flew off.

"Wait!" I yelled, and leaned against the handrail to watch her leave.

And that was when the handrail broke and I fell off the walkway and began to plummet to my death thirty stories below.

# 21

# I CAN'T FLY

There was a rumor in my school that if you ever had a dream in which you were falling off a cliff or a building and in the dream you hit the ground, then in real life you would die right at that moment. I always thought this sounded kinda stupid. I mean, how do you ask people who are already dead if they were dreaming about falling off a cliff and hitting the bottom right before they died? But, just to be safe, whenever I'd have a dream where I was falling I always made extra sure to wake myself up before the end was near.

So to find myself suddenly falling through the air toward the ground below in a world that was completely different from anything I had ever experienced in my life made it sort of hard to remember that I wasn't dreaming.

But I wasn't.

I was scared out of my wits and unhappy about the fact that I really *was* about to die. My body was sort of spinning head over heels so that one minute I was looking at the ground approaching and the next I was looking up at the treetops as they quickly got farther and farther away from me. And it was at that moment that I saw Foo flying down after me like some really pretty version of Superman. Her eyes were wide with fear and surprise. I'd say they were probably as wide as mine but since she knew she could fly and wouldn't herself be dying that day, I'm guessing my face was more panicked than hers. But to see her flying toward me, I had a sudden glimmer of hope that I was about to be saved.

"Iggy!" she yelled as she reached out for me. "I've got you!"

She grabbed me with her hand by the front of my shirt. Unfortunately, we both quickly discovered that flying people's lightweight bodies mean they can't really fly when they're holding anything heavier than them. Especially when that heavy thing is already falling really fast. Like I told you earlier, I'm not fat or anything but compared to Foo, I might as well have weighed as much as an elephant. Foo screamed this high-pitched noise that sort of sounded like the scream my cousin Ernie's parrot makes when it's hungry and nobody's paying attention to it. And the minute

I heard her scream I knew that, once again, I was pretty much about to die.

I looked down and saw that the ground was only about thirty feet away now and I tried to imagine what it was going to feel like to get killed. Would I know that I hit the bottom and feel some huge pain and then everything would go black? Or would I hit and feel myself spatter all over the place and still be alive even though I was dead so that I would just be lying all over the place in a thousand painful pieces that all hurt worse than the time Ivan accidentally slammed my fingers in his mom's car door? Whichever option it was, I wasn't very happy about having to die at that moment.

I looked up at Foo just because I figured if I was about to bite the big one, I might as well do it while looking at someone pretty and nice. I had finally met a girl who it seemed there was a possible chance might like me and now I was going to die before I ever got to know what it's like to have a nice, beautiful girlfriend. Really not fair. And so I might as well enjoy it while I can, I thought, even if it's only for about two more seconds.

I saw Foo's face go from being scared to suddenly looking surprised. And that was when I heard it.

**_KROOOOOSH!!!_**

It was the sound of something popping up out of the leaves and twigs and grass and dirt that were all over the ground. And the next thing I knew I felt these really soft ropes hit my back and form around me like the hammock in my grandma's backyard. And then I felt Foo land right on top of me. She screamed again, but the scream was cut in half as she got the wind knocked out of her when our chests slammed together.

Everything was suddenly quiet. All I could hear was the two of us breathing really hard and fast, like we had both just run the one-mile race on Field Day. I couldn't see much because Foo's wings were still on my face, but I could feel how soft they were.

"Are you all right?" I asked her, unsure what to say after what we had just been through. Plus, I was really worried that maybe she *wasn't* all right.

"Yes," she said, still trying to catch her breath. "Are you okay?"

"I think so," I said as I tried to take stock of my body to feel if I had any pains that might mean something bad had happened. And if I did have some injury, I hoped it wasn't somewhere that Foo could see it. It was embarrassing enough to have her try to save me and almost get killed without then having to be all hurt and probably start crying because I'm not very tough when it comes to getting injured.

"What happened?" I asked as Foo lifted her head and looked around.

"They built a safety net system when Karen started living here. They were afraid that the railing would break someday and she would fall."

"Did she?" I asked, hoping more than anything that Foo's answer would be yes. I really didn't want to be the first idiot to fall out of the treetop city.

"No," said Foo. "You're the first one."

Oh, man. How embarrassing.

We heard a meow.

"What was that?" asked Foo.

"Oh. I think that's just my cat . . . dog . . . thing," I said, not really sure what to call it. We both looked down through the net and saw the cat who thought it was a dog ten feet below us looking up from the ground, wagging its tail.

I turned and looked back at Foo. It was only then that both she and I seemed to realize at the exact same moment that she, a very pretty girl, was lying on top of *me*, a sort of dorky guy, and that our faces were close together enough to either tell each other a secret or to kiss. I can't speak for how this affected her but I can tell you that it made my brain suddenly explode. My heart started pounding like some tiny person with a sledgehammer was trapped inside my chest and was trying to break through the inside of my rib cage to escape.

Foo sort of looked embarrassed that she was on top of me but also didn't jump up to get off of me, either, the way I imagine any other girl I've known in my life would if they ended up anywhere near this close to me. Instead, she raised herself up on her arms and looked at me again.

"You're lumpy," she said with a bit of a smile.

Before I could panic too much about exactly what she might mean by that, she started lightly poking my chest and shoulders with her fingers, the way you might touch a bed to see how soft it was.

"Is everyone from your world as heavy and solid as you?" she asked innocently. I could imagine somebody who wasn't as skinny as I was taking that as an insult, but in my short time knowing Foo, I knew she was usually not being mean or sarcastic when she asked those kinds of questions.

"Yeah, pretty much," I said, still very very aware that she was on top of me. "Most people are way heavier than I am. And there's some guys who are what they call 'bodybuilders' and they're so solid because of all their huge muscles that they become professional wrestlers and then they can hit each other with metal folding chairs and wooden tables and not even get hurt. Although most people think stuff like that is fake. Wrestling, that is."

She was staring at me strangely as I continued my rambling explanation of professional wrestling while I kept asking myself why I was telling her all this. It was like my brain was so desperate not to freak out about having her so close to me that it told my mouth to just come up with whatever it could, no matter how insane it was, just to fill the air with words so that she wouldn't suddenly decide to get off me and end this extremely great moment in my life.

And it was my fear of her getting up that made me completely unprepared for what she did next.

Foo suddenly held out her hand and gently touched my face, starting at my chin, then brushing her hand lightly over my nose, then across my cheek to my ear, then running her open hand with its long thin fingers up over my eyes and across my forehead, and finally putting her fingers right through my hair. Her face had a slightly perplexed expression, the way you might look if you were trying to figure out what something you were touching was made of. I tried to keep a normal look on my face as if this kind of thing happened to me every day back in my frequency, but the guy with the sledgehammer inside my chest was now using a really huge and powerful jackhammer as he blasted away.

And that was when I heard the voice yell, "FOO!"

Suddenly, Foo jumped like somebody had just shot off a gun behind us and her wings slapped all over my face as she flew off me in a panic. I quickly sat up, too, but because the net I was in was so soft and had so many holes in it I couldn't do much other than thrash around like a goldfish that had jumped out of its bowl.

I saw Herfta and his flying sidekicks speeding through the air toward us from the treetops and Karen staring down at me from the walkway high above as Foo hovered about ten feet over me.

Two of the flying guys came down and looked me over to make sure I was all right as I heard Herfta start *puh*ing and *pah*ing like crazy at Foo. I couldn't tell what he was saying but it sounded like he was really mad. She kept gesturing toward me with her arms, then pointing up at the treetops, then back at me and the net and I assumed she was telling him what had just happened. But Herfta kept interrupting her and talking in the soft flying-people language so forcefully and angrily that I expected him to just start yelling really loudly in English the way Mr.

Gilley, my insane math teacher, did whenever he heard anybody talking in class after he had already warned us to "keep our lousy mouths shut."

Finally, Foo nodded and stopped trying to explain and then turned and looked at me with sort of a sad, embarrassed look on her face. Herfta looked at me, too, then gestured to Foo to go back up to the treetop city. She nodded and flew back up super fast, like she was trying to disappear off the face of the earth. Then Herfta flew down next to me.

"Are you all right?" he asked in a tone that sounded like he didn't really care.

"Yes," I said nervously.

"Good. If I ever catch you with my daughter again, I'll personally throw you off the walkway. And this time I guarantee there won't be any safety net to catch you. Got it?"

I nodded yes, feeling a hot flash of panic run up the back of my neck.

Wow, the first girl who ever liked me and now her dad wants to kill me.

This is officially a day of firsts, I thought to myself.

# 22

## UH OH . . .

I had a hard time falling asleep that night. It would have been hard enough to sleep just dealing with the fact that I was trapped in a new world and wasn't sure if I would see my family and friends ever again. And it would have been just as hard to fall asleep thinking about Foo and how pretty she was and the way she touched my face. But add to that the fact that I now knew Herfta was her dad and that the guy hated me *and* (and this is a big *and*) threatened to *kill* me even though I hadn't done anything wrong, and you have all the makings of an extremely sleepless night.

None of this was helped by the fact that I was now sleeping in some really small room that wasn't really even a room but was more like some kind of rickety broom closet made out of sticks. And that I had to sleep on what was pretty much a pile of grass with a ratty old blanket thrown over the top. *And* that I was lonely and wished that the cat had stayed here to keep me company instead of running off into the woods like some big chicken when Herfta and his gang came down to get me.

In my brain I could still hear the *whoosh* of the wooden bowl elevator thingie as it pulled me back up to the treetop city after Herfta had threatened me and how Karen got all mad at me for making Herfta so angry. The more I thought about it the angrier I got. Karen wouldn't believe that I hadn't done anything with Foo and that what had happened in the net was all Foo's doing. I had gotten so mad at Karen for accusing me of being a liar that I called her sort of a rude name and then stormed away and quickly realized I had no place to sleep. And so I told one of Herfta's men that I needed a room and he stuck me in this crappy place. And now I was supposed to get a good night's sleep?

Fat chance.

Since I didn't have a watch and since my cell phone was dead, I don't really know what time I fell asleep. But I do know that once I finally did, I slept that really heavy sleep that you do when you're way more tired than you thought you were when you got in bed. The last time I slept like that was after my dad made me clean out the garage all day and I fell asleep in the backseat of our car on the way home from dinner and the next thing I knew I was still in the backseat and it was morning. When I came in for breakfast, my mom said she and my dad thought it would be better to let me sleep in the car than to wake me up to go to my bedroom, which sort of made me feel like Gary's deadbeat uncle Al who used to fall asleep on their front porch. They'd leave him there all night and he'd sleep so deeply that once a bunch of kids covered him with toilet paper and Silly String at two o'clock in the morning and he didn't even wake up.

As I slept, I dreamed that I was lying in my living room at home and there was a big party going on with all my parents and relatives and friends and they were having a great time around me but I couldn't get up or talk or even move so that I could join the party. At first they were telling me to get up but after I didn't move for a while, they just started putting their drinks and paper plates on me and using me like a coffee table. Then Ivan spilled a scalding hot chocolate all over my stomach and I was trying to scream but couldn't and all of a sudden there was a pounding on our front door and everybody started running because it was the police and they were pounding on the door harder and harder and harder and the room started shaking and all my mom's ceramic animals and dolls that she had on shelves around our living room starting falling and breaking and all of a sudden I woke up and discovered that the pounding and shaking wasn't just in my dream.

The whole room *was* shaking.

Dust and twigs and leaves were falling from the ceiling down on top of me. I heard yelling and wings flapping and birdlike screeches and it sounded like there was a major panic going on outside. Before I could even jump out of bed, Karen stuck her head into the room from outside. She had a look on her face that said something really bad was happening.

And it was.

"They're here!" she yelled at me.

"Who's here?" I asked, feeling all shaky from having woken up so fast.

"Arthur's army! They're trying to destroy the city."

"What city?"

"THIS city!" And with that, Karen disappeared again.

A big **boom** shook the room so violently that I fell out of my bed. Completely off balance and tripping over my feet because my body hadn't fully woken up yet, I jumped up and ran out the door after Karen. The minute I got outside there was another huge explosion and I fell against the building. Suddenly worried that I might fall off the walkway *again*, I crouched down on my hands and knees, crawled to the edge, and looked down.

Around the base of the trees, I saw a massive swarm of creatures wearing the uniforms of Mr. Arthur's army. It looked like there were thousands of them spread out in all directions. Every tree had at least ten or twenty creatures around it swinging axes and hitting the trunks with anything that could cut the trees down.

At the bottom of my tree, which had the biggest and thickest trunk, I saw the creatures stuffing what looked like explosives into a huge hole that they had chopped into its base. The creatures then all ran back and **BOOM!** An explosion of wood and smoke and debris blew out of the hole, knocking the creatures off their feet.

The whole tree shook again like a giant had just kicked it with his huge foot. The walkway jolted and I was thrown up and back against the building again. However, since the walls of the building were only made out of twigs, I crashed halfway through it and found myself practically impaled by some thicker branches that were in the lower half of the wall.

I looked up and saw tons of flying people in the sky, looking completely freaked out and confused. I struggled to my feet and heard a massive cracking sound as the tree slowly started to tip sideways. I could hear all kinds of stuff inside the building fall over and start sliding and rolling across the floors. And then *I* started to slide down the walkway. I grabbed onto the wall and held on as I saw that the building on top of the tree next to us was getting closer. At first I thought it was moving toward us but then I quickly realized that we were falling toward it.

All kinds of things like plates and cups and chairs started tumbling into me and falling over the edge of the walkway. Tons of flying people started pouring out of both buildings and into the sky the same way that crows fly out of a tree when you blow up a huge firecracker next to it. And then, all of a sudden . . . *CRASH!*

Our tree smashed into the other tree. The buildings plowed into each other like two enormous cars hitting head-on. The sound was deafening. The wall I was holding on to exploded outward from the impact and I was suddenly sliding down the walkway holding on to two short branches that used to be part of the wall, getting tons of splinters in my butt in the process.

I looked and saw I was about to slide over the edge of the walkway, this time without much hope of being saved by the safety net and very likely to plunge down on top of a bunch of creatures thirty stories below. Just as I was about to become airborne, I flipped over onto my stomach and stabbed the two branches I was holding into the walkway floor like tent stakes. They hooked over a support branch and I jerked to a stop, almost tearing my arms out of their sockets. My entire body was now hanging over the edge of the walkway as I struggled to hold on to the two branches, which wasn't easy since I was now holding up the entire weight of my body with only my hands and wrists.

This was not a very good position for me to be in, since I had been about the worst member of my gym class and I was especially bad at chin-ups. When we took the President's Physical Fitness Test last semester, they said we had to do five chin-ups and I was only able to do one. And I was only able to do that one because I used my legs to climb up the wall and so they didn't even give me credit for it. So now, to find myself hanging off the side of a tree by my hands, thirty stories above the ground, was just a little more than completely ironic. It might have even been a bit funny if it wasn't me who was about to die.

It was right then that I felt a hand grab onto my wrist, and suddenly I was yanked up and back onto the walkway, where I was face-to-face with Karen.

"We have to get out of here," she said, stating the obvious.

**BOOM!** The tree shook from another explosion down below. I almost fell over the side again but Karen quickly reached out and grabbed the back of my pants, pulling my underwear all the way up my butt crack, giving me a hugely painful but lifesaving wedgie.

Then we heard a loud, deep groan.

We both looked and saw that the building on our treetop and the one it smashed into were starting to slide off their bases and were about take Karen and me with them in the process.

We looked at each other.

"RUN!" Karen yelled.

We started running up the walkway to get out of the path of the quickly crumbling buildings, hoping that the walkway wouldn't also be pulled down in the process. The walls started buckling and branches broke with a noise like gunshot blasts and exploded out at us as we ran past the disintegrating walls. The walkway started to shift and roll like ocean waves as we tried to get to the highest point. What we were going to do once we got there, I had no idea.

We saw up ahead that the tree in front of us was now having *its* trunk assaulted by Arthur's army. Flying people started pouring out of that building, and the sky above was completely filled with thousands of soaring, panicking bodies.

"Why is Mr. Arthur's army doing this?!" I yelled as we ran and dodged exploding branches.

"Because of *us*!" she yelled back as we jumped over a gap in the walkway where about two feet of it had fallen away. "Someone must have followed us yesterday."

"And so they're destroying the whole city? The flying people don't even care about Mr. Arthur. Why would he do this?"

"Because he's a freakin' *psycho*, that's why!"

**CRACK!** The walkway ahead of us suddenly collapsed. Karen and I were barely able to stop ourselves and teetered on the edge before finally falling backward and grabbing onto the still-shaking walkway. And then with a deafening roar, the buildings tore off their bases and tumbled away from us and off the treetop. They smashed against the other trees as they fell and exploded into a downpour of plummeting debris that all the army creatures below scattered to avoid.

"What do we do now?" I asked Karen, probably sounding a little more demanding than I meant to.

"I don't know, I don't know," she said impatiently, as if my question were the last thing she needed to hear at that moment.

Karen looked around and I could see her thinking as she tried to figure out the impossible task of getting us off this tree and down to the ground. Having no idea what to do myself, I pretty much just stood there and rooted for Karen's brain to have a great idea. I wish I could say I was more helpful in that moment, but there are times in life when it seems like there's simply nothing you can do except stand there and hope someone else will save you. It's not a very good thing to admit, since I like to think that there's always some way to get yourself out of a jam. But at this moment, it sure didn't seem like there was a whole lot to be done since neither of us had the power of flight.

Even though I was fearing for my own life, I couldn't help but feel terrible for all the flying people. I mean, it was great that they could fly and at least get away from the attack on their world. But the city had been such a beautiful and peaceful place, with all the buildings and decorations and designs everywhere, and now it had become the most nonpeaceful place I'd ever seen. I kept seeing buildings here and there sway and fall into the trees next to them, and in other places I'd hear an explosion and a building would drop from sight, as if some of the explosives were simply blowing away the whole bottoms of the trees they were on.

Karen looked up and saw something, which made me look up just in time to see a bunch of flying people heading down toward us.

"They're coming to help us!" I yelled.

"Uh . . ." said Karen as she stared up at them. "I don't think they're coming to *help* us."

She was right. Because suddenly three of them swooped down and started hitting us with their wings and slapping at us with their lightweight hands as the rest hovered behind them and stared at us like they wanted to kill us.

"*FAH PAH COO TOO CAR TOM TEE!*" yelled a flying woman and her friends as they attacked Karen.

Karen yelled back at them in their puh-pah language and sounded both angry and apologetic at the same time, like a girl who knew she had done something wrong but who didn't like the fact that she was getting punished for it.

The flying woman yelled, "*CHAM PUT!*" and they all flew away, throwing one final angry look back at us.

"What was *that* about?" I asked as I tried to catch my breath.

"What do you think?" Karen said, suddenly sounding completely depressed. "We destroyed their city. It's our fault for leading Arthur's army here." Her eyes then started to get all glassy and she stared out at the disintegrating tree-top city, looking like she was going to cry. "It's *my* fault."

I never know what to do if a girl starts crying and usually end up making some sort of halfhearted gesture along the lines of saying, "Don't worry, it'll be okay," and giving them an awkward pat on the arm. And today was no exception.

"Don't worry," I said as I awkwardly reached out to pat her arm. "It'll be o —"

## BOOM!

Karen and I were knocked off our feet as the tree we were leaning against shook violently and then started to slowly tip over, which meant that our tree started to tip with it. No, things were not going to be okay.

Things were about to be terrible.

**23**

## OUT OF THE
## FRYING PAN . . .

As the two trees groaned and cracked and started to fall over and Karen and I tried to hold on to the walkway to keep from sliding off it and plunging several hundred feet to "meet our maker," as my grandma used to say when somebody died, we both heard a voice yell, "IGGY!"

We looked up and saw Foo hovering right above us. She was holding a rope. I looked and saw that it stretched behind her and was tied to the walkway of the next tree over. She threw it down to us and yelled, "JUMP!"

As soon as the rope hit us, Karen and I grabbed onto it and quickly realized that it was going to be a bit awkward for both of us to swing on the rope at the same time. However, the only option other than "awkward" was "dead," and so we grabbed the rope together and hung on tight. That turned out to be a good thing because there was a super loud **CRACK!** and the tree we were on plunged out from under our feet and crashed to the ground.

Karen and I were suddenly airborne, falling as we both screamed and clung even tighter to the rope. I felt Karen's legs wrap around my knees as she tried to get herself as securely fastened to the rope as possible. Her leg muscles were so strong that I thought she was going to break my kneecaps.

It felt like we were falling forever, even though it was probably only a few seconds. Then suddenly I felt the rope go taut and we started swinging toward the tree that the rope was tied to like two out-of-control Tarzans. I think I was screaming pretty loudly because I remember Karen saying, "You're hurting my ears," but you'd be screaming, too, if you were me, since I was facing the tree and could see that we were seconds away from smashing directly into it and getting impaled on all its little sharp thorns. And while I was grateful to Foo for helping us out with the rope and all, I couldn't help feeling like she hadn't really thought out the entire plan.

We started to turn as we swung and Karen suddenly had a view of what I was screaming about.

"Iggy," she yelled, "hold out your feet and push us past the tree when we hit it."

"Me?" I yelled back. "My legs aren't strong enough. You do it!"

"Oh, God, you're such a wuss! We're going too fast. We'll both have to do it."

We were almost at the tree and swinging in rapidly. Way too rapidly for our legs to do much other than break and get perforated by the thorns. But since we had no other options, we both held out our feet and waited for what we knew was going to be a majorly painful and potentially catastrophic collision.

And that was when I realized that Foo actually *had* thought out her plan a bit more than I'd assumed she had.

Out of nowhere, Foo swooped in carrying a big piece of the soft foamy material that had stopped me from breaking my head at the top of the wooden elevator bowl thing and held it up against the tree right before we hit. Karen and I thumped hard against the soft foam and, while it didn't keep our collision from hurting, it padded us enough to keep us from breaking our legs and getting killed by all the hard, sharp thorns.

We bounced off the foam and then swung back and forth for a little while like the pendulum on a grandfather clock until we finally stopped midair, dangling several hundred feet above the forest floor.

"Oh, man," I said. The skin on my hands felt like it was on fire. "I don't know how much longer I can hang on."

"Geez, do you always complain like an old lady?" Karen said, her voice showing that she didn't have a lot more hanging-on time left in her, either. "All you ever do is tell me all the stuff you can't do. Do you ever talk about the stuff you *can* do?"

"Yeah. Right now, I *can* let go of the rope and fall. I *can* enjoy not being yelled at by you for once. And I *can* tell you that we'd better think of some way to get back down onto the ground because we're not gonna have any more trees to hide in soon."

Before Karen could respond, Foo flew up and hovered next to us.

"No one will help me carry you guys away," Foo said, sounding a bit too calm for my taste. "They're all mad at you. And I'd need at least ten of us to carry your weight." Then Foo looked up above us. "I can lower you both down to the ground but then you'd be right in the middle of the army."

Foo pointed down at the thousands of creatures swarming around all the trees who were continuing to chop and blow up the tree trunks. It didn't look like a good place for us to go.

"Hey, it's either that or fall on top of them from up here and die," said Karen, stating the very thing I knew but was afraid to admit. "Just get us off this rope."

Foo gave us a worried look, then looked me in the eyes, reached out, and touched my face with her hand. Even though I was in a really dangerous situation at that moment, my heart sort of leaped in my chest again. Hey, when a pretty girl touches your face, it's a really big deal, no matter what you happen to be doing at the moment.

Foo flew up to the walkway. We saw that she had tied the rope we were on to the rail that was next to another wooden elevator bowl. She pushed the lever and the bowl started to come slowly down next to us. When it stopped, Karen swung her feet up and got inside the bowl, then pulled the rope closer so that I could get into it.

**BOOM!** The tree shook and the bowl bounced. We looked down and saw a huge cloud of smoke where the explosion had just occurred. It had taken a pretty big chunk out of our tree, though not enough to make it fall over. But the explosion had made all the creatures run away from the bottom of it.

"Okay," said Karen. "It's now or never." She looked up at Foo. "Drop us!"

Foo nodded and hit the lever.

**SHOOM!** The bowl dropped so fast that I thought my stomach was going to fly out of my mouth. We plummeted so rapidly that the tree next to us just looked like a blur, and then all of a sudden, the bowl jerked to a stop inside the cloud from the explosion. Karen and I slammed together as we both fell over from the impact. I waited for her to yell at me but her kung fu brain was already getting ready for our escape.

"All right," she said through the smoke, which was making us both cough. "Follow me and don't let anybody attack me from behind. Just grab something and start swinging it."

Karen jumped out of the bowl and I watched through the smoke as she grabbed a big jagged shaft of wood that had been blown off of the tree. I jumped out after her and reached down for some kind of weapon. The first thing I grabbed was a really long, thin branch. I wanted to look for something stronger but Karen was already running out of the smoke and yelling, "Iggy! C'mon!"

I pulled my book bag off my back, figuring that it might be a better weapon than a long skinny stick, followed her out of the smoke, and immediately realized that we were in major trouble. We were completely surrounded by Mr. Arthur's army. All of the tough mole guys and three-legged no-armed gorillas and purple babies and praying mantises and giant potato bugs and fly-headed octopuses stared at us with bloodthirsty looks. The gorilla guys all had giant swords that they would hold up to the side with one of their feet and then toss back and forth, always putting the feet that weren't holding the sword back down on the ground so that they kind of looked like they were hopping as they brandished their weapons. But it wasn't the kind of hopping that was funny. It was the kind of hopping that said we were about to get our heads chopped off.

They all started moving in on Karen and me. Karen held up her jagged piece of wood as I put my back against hers and wished that somehow I could just meld into her so that she could protect me and I wouldn't have to try and fight off Mr. Arthur's army with the book bag and crappy long twig I was holding. But I honestly didn't see how even Karen could fight her way out of this one. I mean, I'd seen Bruce Lee movies where he beat up about twenty guys at one time but I don't think even Bruce Lee could fight his way out of the middle of a thousand huge, armed creatures.

Man, at that moment I was sure hoping that Karen was a lot tougher than Bruce Lee.

# 24

## . . . INTO THE FIRE

"Iggy," Karen whispered over her shoulder at me. "Make your cell phone ring again."

"I can't," I whispered back. "The battery's dead."

"Why'd you leave it on?!" she whispered back angrily.

"I didn't!" I whispered back again, figuring that maybe lying would keep me from getting yelled at during this tense moment. "I have a bad battery."

"You came to another frequency with a bad battery?"

"It's not like I knew I was coming!"

"Well, we're gonna be as dead as your battery in about two seconds," she said as she looked at the creatures who were glaring at us and slowly moving in.

"Can't you fight our way out of here?"

"Who the hell do you think I am?" she whispered incredulously. "Bruce Lee?"

Oh, man. We were so dead.

*WHAP!* Suddenly a big piece of netting dropped down on top of the group of gorilla guys who were standing in front of Karen. We looked up and saw Foo swooshing past. She looked down and gave me a smile and a nod that seemed to say, "There you go. Now you can fight your way out of there."

The gorilla guys sort of freaked out the minute the net hit them. The front two threw their feet-hands up in the air to fight with the net and dropped their swords on the ground. Karen and I saw this and got the same idea.

"Grab the swords!" we both yelled at the exact same time. Normally if that happened, I'd yell something stupid like "Jinx!" or "Buy me a Coke!" because that's what you're supposed to yell if two people say the exact same thing at the exact same time. But clearly this wasn't the right moment. Even a goofball like me knew that.

We both dived for the swords and grabbed them. They were super heavy and I sort of had to drag mine until my arm figured out just how much the thing weighed and got used to it. But Karen had hers up and was pointing its sharp tip at the creatures with a look on her face that said, "Okay, who wants their head cut off first?"

Making sure nobody was coming up behind us, I looked back and saw the wooden elevator bowl and suddenly got an idea. I didn't know if it was a good idea but at that moment my options were a) have a sword fight with a thousand huge army guys from another frequency even though I had never had a sword fight before in my life or b) think of some other way out of this. And so my idea seemed like the way to go.

I ran over to the bowl and with a swing of the sword cut the ropes the bowl was hanging on. The bowl thumped onto the ground as I turned and called to Karen.

"Hey!" I yelled, pointing at the bowl. "Turtle tank!"

Karen gave me as weird a look as you probably are right now because neither of you would know what "turtle tank" is. But I did because of this really stupid game that Ivan, Gary, and I used to play. We'd take Ivan's blue plastic swimming pool from when he was really little and two of us would turn it upside down and then get under it. Then we'd have to run with our legs all crouched so that we sort of looked like a big blue headless turtle. Whoever wasn't under the pool had to try to stop us before we got to the opposite fence in Ivan's backyard. It was a pretty dumb game and something we stopped playing after Ivan got a baseball bat without telling us and hit the pool so hard as we were running at him that he knocked one of Gary's teeth out and made my ears ring for about three days. But we always found that it was sort of hard to stop whoever was under the pool from running past just because the thing was so big.

The wooden bowl was smaller than the pool but was higher and rounder and seemed like something Karen and I could use to get through the crowd, since it was hard enough to protect us from swinging swords and axes.

I grabbed the bowl and tipped it to show Karen

w h a t

I was talking about. She seemed to understand and got a skeptical look.

"You're joking, righ —?"

**RIIPPPPP!** The gorilla guys tore through the net and pulled it apart, now madder than they were before Foo dropped the net on them. They raised their remaining swords and started to charge at us.

"Let's do it!" Karen yelled as she ran toward me.

We grabbed the bowl and flipped it over on top of us. I didn't hunch over low enough and got clonked on the head really hard.

"Ow!" I yelled.

"Shut up and lift it with your shoulders!"

"Hey, don't tell me how to do a turtle tank! It was my idea."

"Then GO!"

We heaved the heavy wooden bowl up on our backs and started to run right at the gorilla guys. Immediately, we heard tons of swords hitting the bowl and felt them pushing against us as they tried to stop us. We could see their weird feet-hands poking under the bowl as they swarmed around us and then we saw some of the feet grab the sides of the bowl as they tried to lift it off us.

"Use your sword!" Karen yelled so that I could hear her over the deafening sound of swords hitting us. She then took her sword and swept it fast along the bottom edge of the bowl. *SWIP!* The sword neatly cut off the fingers of a foot-hand that was holding on. Blood spurted out of it as we heard a scream and the foot-hand quickly pulled away. I thought I was going to faint. I've never been good around blood or anything gross and I even passed out once when they showed a movie in our science class about how to do CPR. So seeing something get its fingers and/or toes cut off right in front of me was a bit more than my sensitive brain could handle. But, fortunately or unfortunately, when a thousand huge creatures are trying to kill you, there's not a lot of time for fainting.

Karen and I started running even faster as she used her sword to stab at the feet of any creatures that came too close. I tried to do the same but since I was behind Karen, I was worried that I might end up stabbing her in the foot or cutting off her leg with my sword if I moved it from side to side too much. And so I just tried to stab down on the right side of the bowl as if I were skiing and the sword was one of my ski poles.

It was at this moment I realized we couldn't see where the heck we were going. We were getting through the crowd pretty effectively but it was only a matter of time before we ran into a tree. Which is exactly what happened next.

**THWACK!**

Karen smacked into the front of the bowl and I smacked into her back, hitting so hard we clunked our heads together for the second time in twenty-four hours. We fell down and the bowl whumped onto the ground around us, creating a safety shell over our bodies. We then heard swords and axes start chopping at the bowl again as we both tried to recover from the collision.

"This is stupid," Karen said, sounding like she was in major pain as we sat in the dark wooden igloo. "We can't even see where we're going. This is no way to fight."

"It's either this or get killed," I said, hoping that Karen wasn't about to do what I had a feeling she was about to do.

"Iggy, look. These guys are all terrible fighters because they never even held swords before Mr. Arthur put them up to it. So just start swinging that blade and look mean and scream a lot and you'll scare the life out of most of them. And then follow me. I know a way out of this forest."

"Wait a minute. What do you mean I'll scare 'most' of them?"

But it was too late. Karen flipped the bowl off us and let out the loudest battle yell I'd ever heard in my life. I looked up and saw we were surrounded by a ton of army creatures and that they were all suddenly just standing there staring at us in complete shock. And then Karen lifted the sword over her head, yelled again, and charged right into the middle of them. The creatures all scattered as if she were carrying a bomb that was about to go off, and I watched her disappear through the dense crowd. Then they all turned and looked back at me.

Oh, man.

I took a deep breath, jumped up, yelled as loud as I could, then lifted my sword and ran straight at them.

Nobody moved.

Two of the gorilla guys stuck out their feet-hands and grabbed my arms. A praying mantis guy reached out and snatched the sword out of my hand. Then the gorilla guys spun me around and pulled me against them, taking their swords and putting the sharp edges up against my neck.

Apparently these guys were not in the "scare the life out of most of them" category.

The creatures facing me all smiled and looked like they were going to eat me for breakfast. They held up their weapons and I suddenly knew what a Thanksgiving turkey must feel like when it's lying on the chopping block. I looked up and saw Foo hovering high above, staring down at me with a helpless look on her face.

The crowd of creatures parted and the huge mole guy who had tried to capture us back in Karen's hideout pushed through them. Seeing his fancy uniform up against those of the other creatures, I could tell that he was the head of the army. He stared at me with an angry look, then made what I assumed was a smile for mole people, since it was sort of hard to tell exactly what part of his weird round mouth were the sides that are supposed to go up to form a smile.

"Mr. Arthur wants to see you," said the mole guy's deep rumbling voice. "And I sure wouldn't want to be you right now."

That made two of us.

# 25

## SLAPPING THE PRESIDENT FIVE

As I marched along like a prisoner in the middle of Mr. Arthur's army and felt the various swords and weapons poking against the book bag on my back, I could still hear the explosions and chopping behind us as the creatures continued to cut down the flying people's treetop city. I had thought they would stop once they found Karen and me, but for some reason they were dead set on destroying the flying people's home. It made me wonder all the more about how insane and evil Mr. Arthur must have become in his time away from our frequency.

Was he this loony and heartless back when he was a teacher in our school? Did these feelings lurk inside him as he taught his classes, like some kind of flu germ you catch that doesn't show its symptoms for a few days? Or did the journey from our frequency to this one make him crazy? Did he start out normal, feeling the same feelings I did when I first arrived, and then slowly the craziness took him over and he lost his mind? Or had he always been a bad guy who was just looking for a good place to be bad? I had no idea but I had a feeling I was about to find out.

The army marched me through the middle of Lesterville like I was the grand marshal in a parade. The only difference was that normally people *like* the grand marshal in a parade. For me, all the creatures came out and lined the streets of the fake Times Square and booed and hissed and made all the sounds that their various species made to show their disapproval of something or someone. In this case, me.

Now, as you know, I had never been very popular back in my frequency but I had never been booed before. I had seen criminals on TV doing what the news called "the perp walk" (perp being short for perpetrator) and people had booed them, but those were guys who had killed people and done all sorts of horrible things. I was just some kid who got thrown into a different world and apparently befriended somebody the creatures here really didn't like. It seemed like an overreaction, if you ask me. Of course, since there were so many army guys with me, maybe the creatures felt they had to boo to keep from getting arrested themselves. Who could tell?

We marched past the theater where Hamlet was playing and I realized I was now heading into a part of the city I had never seen before. It looked pretty much as fake and crummy as the rest of the city looked, with the addition of a huge statue of Mr. Arthur in the middle of a park that was filled with rickety swing sets that little mole kids were trying to swing on but kept falling off because they don't really have butts.

I knew the statue was of Mr. Arthur because *everything* in this place was about Mr. Arthur. But I have to say, it was a pretty terrible statue. It sort of looked more like a mannequin in a department store and the face seemed like something I might draw if somebody made me draw a picture of Mr. Arthur using only my left hand. And since I'm right-handed, you can only imagine what that would look like. But as weird as that statue was, it wasn't until we rounded the corner that I saw something that really threw me for a loop.

The White House.

There it was, sitting at the end of a really big lawn surrounded by a huge fence that looked like the fence around the real White House but that was way taller and scarier. It was the kind of fence you would never try to climb over because you knew you'd get impaled on the spikes at the top or caught by guards before you were even halfway up it.

There were tons of guards from all the different creature species dressed in poorly fitting suits positioned along the fence, and I had to figure Mr. Arthur was hoping the suits would make them look like secret service men. Unfortunately for him, they just looked more like when people have a pet parade and dress their dogs and cats up in human clothes and costumes. The creatures he had chosen were mean-looking, but their clothes sort of made you want to burst out laughing and say, "Awwww, isn't that cute?"

We came up to a guardhouse at the front gate. The mole guy commander and the two gorilla guards walked me up to a giant purple baby who was dressed in an enormous dark suit with a tie that was way too short.

"Got the new Anti-Art," said the mole guy in his deep rumble. "President Arthur wanted him brought in as soon as we caught him."

"Good work," said the purple baby in a weird voice that I can only describe as something the world's biggest munchkin might have. He then did a big salute. *RIIIPPPP!* The armpit of his suit split open. "Oh, man," was all he said as he looked at the hole he had just made and stared at his armpit like he was going to cry.

We marched up the driveway that led to the White House and I was surprised to see that it actually looked pretty real and well built. I figured that Mr. Arthur probably put a lot more time and care into building the place he lived in than he did into the stuff he just had to look at as he passed by. After all, if I was going to be a crazy dictator and force a whole frequency of creatures to do my bidding and recreate my entire world from back home, I'd probably build my house well, too. I mean, who wants to live in a piece of junk?

We walked up between the tall columns in the front and the mole commander knocked on the door. A feel (one of those fish/eel-type creatures that was standing in line behind the mole guys at Artbucks, in case you forgot) answered the door. He was dressed like a butler in a tuxedo, even though the tuxedo only had one arm that was coming out of the back of the jacket, since that's where feels' arms are. He gave the mole commander a look that showed he didn't like him and said, "Yes?"

"Got the Anti-Art," said the mole commander, who clearly didn't like the feel, either.

"Just give him to me," said the feel, who I now noticed had a really bad version of an English accent. It was weird enough to hear a fish/eel-type creature speaking at all, but when you add a bad British accent on top of it, *and* a tuxedo with one arm, *AND* factor in that we were standing in the doorway of a fake White House, well . . . you get my point that it was weird, right?

"We need to bring him in ourselves," said the mole commander, as if the feel were an idiot for not knowing that.

"*Forget* it," said the feel in the same tone you might use if somebody said they wanted to come into your living room and take a dump on the floor. "You guys aren't stepping one foot into this place."

"I was told to deliver the Anti-Art to President Arthur personally," the mole guy said like he was about three seconds away from hitting the feel.

"And you have, *Commander*." (The feel said the word *commander* in a super sarcastic way.) "Now, give him to me."

The feel reached out his suction cup and was about to stick it on my chest when the mole commander grabbed the feel's arm and yanked it down.

"OW!" the feel yelled.

"Keep your sucker off my prisoner, No Legs!"

"Who you calling No Legs, Dirt-Eater?!"

"Who you calling Dirt-Eater, No Legs?!"

"Who you calling No Legs, Dirt-Eater?!"

"Who you calling Dirt-Eater, No Legs?!"

And with that rather lame exchange they suddenly started shoving each other back and forth like they were about to have a fight on the playground. I thought that maybe I could use this chance to escape when . . .

"ENOUGH!" I heard a voice yell.

The feel and the mole commander stopped fighting and we all looked through the door into the White House. There, in silk pajamas and a red velvet smoking jacket, standing on the top of a big curved staircase in front of a gigantic painting of himself dressed the exact same way, was Mr. Arthur.

"Everybody please stop fighting," he said, less like he was mad and more like he thought the fight was kind of amusing. "Is this the way we act when we have a new guest in our house?"

He came down the stairs and walked over to us. I could see that he was wearing one of those rich-guy scarves around his neck, the kind that you tie and then tuck into the front of your shirt so that it puffs out of your open collar. I think my dad used to call them "ascots." Whatever it was, it sort of made Mr. Arthur look like a cross between Mr. Howell, the rich guy from *Gilligan's Island*, and Hugh Hefner, this old guy who owned a magazine that nobody my age was allowed to see.

"I'm sorry, sir," said the feel as he bowed his head toward Mr. Arthur. "I didn't want to let them in because I know how you don't like any dirt inside the White House."

Mr. Arthur patted the feel on its back to say "it's okay," and then stepped through the doorway. The mole commander and all the army guys bowed their heads as Mr. Arthur stopped and looked me up and down.

"The new Anti-Art, Your Excellency," said the mole commander in a voice that sounded like he was trying to be really nice. "He was hiding in the flappers' city with the girl, as you predicted."

"I take it the girl got away?"

"Yes, sir," said the mole as he bowed his head. "But we'll find her."

"Yes," said Mr. Arthur with a smile. "I know you will."

The mole commander and the entire army bowed over and over again as they backed away from the door. With all the bowing and walking backward I guess the creatures at the back weren't moving fast enough and nobody could see where they were going and suddenly about forty of them, including the mole commander, all crashed into each other and fell backward like dominos. The creatures got mad in their own native languages and it sort of sounded like all the animals at a zoo swearing.

"ARTLISH ONLY, PLEASE!" yelled Mr. Arthur.

The creatures jumped up and backed away toward the fence twice as fast, this time saying, "Sorry, President Arthur!" and "It'll never happen again, Your Excellency!" over each other. Then they all turned and ran out of the White House yard and disappeared down the street.

Mr. Arthur watched all this, then started laughing. "Oh, man, it's funny when they do that." Then he looked at me, got a big smile on his face, and held out his hand, palm up. "I'm Chester Arthur and I'm the president of this place. Give me five, soul man!"

It took me a few seconds to realize that he wanted me to slap him five the old-fashioned way that I used to see my dad do with his friends. But since Mr. Arthur was the president and all *and* since the last time I made direct contact with the hand of a leader from this world I had crushed it, I was a bit nervous to suddenly hit the hand of the guy I had just seen destroy an entire treetop city. However, he just stood there with his hand out and an expectant look on his face, which he then followed up by saying, "Don't leave me hangin'."

Unsure if the offense of leaving him "hangin'" would result in an even worse punishment than the one I was already expecting for befriending Karen, I very carefully raised my hand and slapped his excellency five.

"All *riiiight!*" he said, laughing as he pointed a finger at me and snapped his thumb down like his hand was a gun. "What's your name?"

"Uh . . . Ignatius," I said nervously. "Ignatius Mac-Farland."

"Holy smokes, that's quite a name, man!" he said, laughing again. "You must have gotten teased like crazy back in our frequency. You're from my hometown, right?"

"Yeah."

"Dig it, man. Right on! Hey, how'd you like a tour of the White House, Ignatius MacFarland?"

Wow, I thought. Mr. Arthur is really weird.

# 26

## IN CHESTER WE TRUST

"This, my man, is the main lobby," Mr. Arthur said loudly, like he was giving a tour to a large group of people even though it was only me standing next to him. "The whole idea for a White House came to me in one of my many creative dreams, the same dreams where most of my best ideas come from."

As Mr. Arthur talked, he watched the feel butler move across the lobby floor on its slithering coil and go through a door into another room. As soon as it was gone, Mr. Arthur walked up to me and gave me a playful punch on the arm, like we were the best of friends.

"So what do you think of everything you've seen?" he

said with a look that showed he was sure I was going to say something good.

"It's a nice lobby," I said, a bit confused.

"No, man," he laughed. "My city. My world. You saw all that stuff out there, didn't you?"

"Oh, uh, yeah." I wasn't really quite sure what to say and was sort of hoping he wouldn't ask me any questions like that. My mom had always said, "If you can't say anything nice, then don't say anything at all." Well, I was going to have to be awfully quiet now.

"*So?*" he chuckled. "What did you think of it?"

I wasn't really sure what to do. I didn't want to lie but since this guy was also the president and since he was obviously a person who could do really bad things to someone he didn't like, I felt like I should maybe just tell him I thought all the stuff he had passed off as his own and all the crappy buildings and clothing and stores and everything else he had forced on this frequency were really good. But I just couldn't. I was caught in what you might call a dilemma.

"Well . . ." I said cautiously, "it looks a lot like the stuff back home." It was a vague statement that I said in a sort of upbeat tone and so I hoped he would take it as a compliment.

"Yeah, I know, it looks like stuff back home, but what do you *think* of it?" he said in a voice that clearly showed he wanted me to be all "Wow, it's great!" and "You are the most talented person I've ever met!"

"Well . . ." I said, even more cautiously now as my brain spun trying to figure out the most careful wording possible. "It's pretty amazing. I really can't believe you did it."

Mr. Arthur got a huge smile and then held out his palm for me to slap again. "Thank you, my brother!"

Glad that I seemed to have dodged a bullet, I slapped him a sort of halfhearted five. He did the gun-hand thing at me again and gestured for me to follow him.

"So," he said, in a really good mood, "how'd you get to this frequency?"

"I made a rocket and it blew up with me inside it," I said, a bit embarrassed.

"Whoa, super cool! You're lucky you didn't kill yourself, bro."

"Yeah. I know." It was sort of hard to have a normal conversation with the guy, knowing all that I did about him. After seeing what he had done to the flying people's city, I kept waiting for him to throw me in a dungeon or take a punch at me or pull out a gun and shoot me like the bad guys do in those movies where you think they're nice and then they just suddenly kill a guy because he double-crossed them or stole their money.

Mr. Arthur walked up to a door under the staircase and pushed it open. Then he turned to me and got a smile that said he was going to show me something top secret. "Come on in, rocket man, and see where it all happens."

Oh, man, I thought. Dungeon time. Ice pick in the back of the head. The end of Iggy.

He gestured for me to go through the door. I took a deep breath, tried to tell myself that I could kick him in the nuts like Karen did if things got dangerous, and headed in.

Yikes.

I was suddenly standing in a huge workshop that looked like a bomb had gone off inside it. There were piles of stuff everywhere, mounded all the way up to the ceiling. There were different workstations all around, as well as weird-looking electronics equipment. In one corner, big wooden boxes and cases with lights and wires sticking out and microphones that sort of looked like tennis rackets sat in a circle around a huge collection of homemade musical instruments. Giant easels with lots of half-finished versions of famous paintings like the *Mona Lisa* stood in another corner. A huge desk with mountains of papers and manuscripts and an oversize homemade typewriter that looked like someone had glued a bunch of baby blocks to a cash register sat in the middle of the room.

Everywhere else were various projects in different stages of completeness — a car made out of big sheets of weird-looking metal, a hang glider built out of branches and some kind of rough fabric, an airplane and a helicopter that looked junkier than the rocket I had made. There was even something that looked like a huge bamboo machine gun on a stand that didn't look anywhere near being ready to do any damage other than falling over on whoever tried to shoot it. There wasn't one foot of space that didn't have something piled on it, and I couldn't tell how anybody could even walk through it all to get to the various work areas.

I looked up at Mr. Arthur, who was staring at the room proudly.

"This is where all the magic happens," he said. "This is the place where I make everyone's lives better."

I looked at him, surprised by what he just said. This guy really likes himself, I thought. He looked down at me for a few seconds, like he was trying see inside my head.

"I know what you're thinking," he finally said. "A lot of this is based on stuff from our world. But I'm not stealing the ideas. I'm trying to make them *better*. I'm fixing the things about our frequency's accomplishments that didn't work, that weren't good enough. Like, here, check this out, dude."

Mr. Arthur ran through all the junk like a little kid, leaping over piles and landing each foot in empty spaces that were only big enough for one of his shoes. It was clear that to him this whole layout made sense, just like my dad's desk, which looked like a disaster area to my mom and me but my dad could find even the smallest piece of paper on. "It's my own personal filing system," he used to say whenever my mom would get down on him to clean his desk, even though if the desk in my bedroom was ever messy he would call me a slob and say I was grounded unless I "made sense of that trash heap."

Mr. Arthur grabbed the painting of the *Mona Lisa* off its easel and ran back over.

"See, the *Mona Lisa* in our frequency has this really small smile that you can barely see. In fact, some art scholars even argue about whether or not she's really smiling. But if you look at my version of it, well . . . check it out."

Mr. Arthur pointed at her mouth. It was smiling really big, with huge white teeth and everything.

"Now, that's a smile!" he said, laughing the way a person does when they're just so happy to be themselves. "And listen to this!"

He put the painting down and bounded into the middle of the room and grabbed a guitar that was made out of some kind of green wood and started to play it. As soon as I heard the opening notes, I knew it was a song that I'd heard my dad play on his car radio a million times. He always said it was the most famous rock song ever. After Mr. Arthur plunked out the opening notes, he started to sing in a really high, terrible voice.

*"There's a lady whose nose | knows what glitters is good | and she's climbing a stairway to Kevin."* He stopped playing and looked at me with another one of his "Well, it's pretty great, isn't it?" faces.

"Uh . . ." I said, trying not to insult him, "who's Kevin?"

"See, that's just the thing, brother man," he said, getting all excited and waving his hands around as he talked. "The original song's called 'Stairway to *Heaven*.' But that doesn't make any sense, you know? I mean, there's no stairway that's that tall. And who cares about a woman climbing up to heaven anyway, since if she is, then she's already dead, you know?

"So I made the song more of a story about this girl who's in love with this guy named Kevin who wears really glittery clothes because he's, you know, like, a real cool guy in a rock band and he lives up on the second floor of her apartment building and she's been afraid to talk to him forever. But now she's finally decided that it's time to tell him she loves him and so she's climbing a . . ." He gave me a look and gestured to me to finish the sentence for him.

"Stairway to Kevin," I said, feeling very self-conscious even though it was only the two of us in the room.

"Pretty great, huh?!" he laughed, more pleased with himself than any person has ever been in the history of the universe.

"Yeah," was pretty much all I could say.

Are all presidents like this? I wondered.

# 27

# INSIDE THE OVAL OFFICE

We finally got out of Mr. Arthur's weird workshop, but only after he'd shown me pretty much everything he was working on, which was a *lot* of stuff. He was trying to invent a DVD, build a motorcycle, make hockey equipment, draw Superman comic books, shoot episodes of *The Simpsons*, genetically engineer coffee beans, design a robot — he was even trying to clone himself. The amazing thing was he was a pretty smart guy and was able to do a lot of stuff for being an English teacher. The problem was he was only a *pretty* smart guy and not a *really* smart guy and so he was only able to do stuff halfway right.

I have to admit, it was impressive that he had been able to make the materials he needed for all his projects out of stuff he found in this frequency, since there were no stores that sold electronics equipment or mechanical parts or art supplies or scientific instruments or any of the other materials that you can just buy in our world. But this also created as many problems for him as the fact that he wasn't really smart enough to do all this stuff well. Nothing really worked the way it should have. And so everything he did and made and invented just came off as kind of terrible.

Oh, yeah, and the fact that he also thought everything he was doing was amazing didn't help, either.

We walked down a hallway that looked a lot like the hallways I'd seen on TV programs about the inside of the White House. There was carpeting everywhere and it looked normal but when I walked on it, it sort of made a crunching noise. All I could think about was how uncomfortable it would have been to walk around this place in my bare feet.

We got to a set of double doors and he stopped in front of them.

"You ever been to the White House and visited the President, Iggy Mac?" he said like he could barely contain his excitement.

"No, sir. I've just seen the place on TV."

"Well, you'll never be able to say *that* again!" And with that, he pushed open the doors and revealed the Oval Office, which looked pretty much exactly the way it looked

whenever I'd seen it in movies and on TV and in my government book. It had the couches and desk and chairs and
tables and windows and curtains that were just like the real
place. I have to admit that, of all the stuff I'd seen that Mr.
Arthur had done, this was the only one that looked exactly
right.

He even had a Presidential Seal in the middle of the carpet that looked just like the one in the real White House,
except that it said E PLURIBUS CHESTER, which I think in

Latin means "Out of many, Chester." That doesn't make any sense at all, unless he was trying to say that if you added up all the creatures in this frequency you would get one of him.

"Pretty great, huh?" he said, looking prouder than I'd ever seen anybody look in the twelve and a half years I'd been on the planet Earth.

"Yeah," I said, truly impressed with the place. "It's really cool."

He showed me in and then he sat behind the desk that I'd always seen the President sit at and I sat in one of the two chairs across from it. Mr. Arthur put his feet up on the desk, leaned back, and put his hands behind his head like he was king of the planet. He stared at me for a few seconds, then smiled again and said, "So, Ignatius MacFarland. Welcome to my world."

I didn't know what to say to the guy. He kept acting really normal and friendly toward me and yet the only reason I was there was that he had ordered his army to go and find me and destroy anything that got in their way as they did. So to have a normal conversation with him like we were just sitting around in someone's backyard on a cool summer evening drinking pop and eating potato chips was like trying to calmly eat a sandwich while the car you're riding in is plummeting off the side of a cliff. I wasn't sure how much longer I could do it.

"So, um . . ." I said, looking around the room for some sort of conversation starter, "how long have you been the President?"

"A few years now, I guess. It's sort of hard to remember, to be honest. I've been so busy that I tend to lose track of time. I didn't really invent a calendar or anything because I'd sort of like to forget that time is passing. It's something that happens to you as you start to get older. It's weird. When you're young, like the age you are, time seems like it goes really slowly. But the older you get, the faster it goes. Sometimes it feels like I just got up in the morning and then suddenly it's nighttime and I'm getting back in bed. You have that happen every day for weeks and months and years and then suddenly you look in the mirror and you're an old man because your whole life has passed you by.

"That was how I felt when I was back in our frequency," he continued. "And I hated it. I mean, if you're busy or successful as it's happening, then you don't mind it so much because you feel like you're doing something with your life. But when you're just trying to do things and you keep getting rejected or told that it's not good or you're made to feel like you're just wasting your life chasing some dream that's not attainable, then it's the worst thing in the world."

Mr. Arthur looked at me and thought for a second. Then he got this really serious look on his face and I wondered if it was time for him to tell me I was going to be thrown in the dungeon.

"I'm not gonna lie to you, Iggy. Karen told me everybody back home thought I tried to kill myself when my house blew up. Well, it's true. I did. I hated my life back then. Nobody understood what I was doing. They didn't get what I was trying to do with my writing and with the plays I put on and the music I wrote. They all thought they knew what was good and that I didn't. And so just because they didn't understand how unique my creations were they acted like I was a joke.

"They laughed at me behind my back. And I didn't have enough money to quit my job and move to a place where I would be appreciated. So I decided that I would just get out of that place. And for some reason I ended up here. Now look at me. I'm the freakin' President!"

He held his arms out as a way of saying "Ta da!" I didn't quite know how to react to his story.

"Uh . . . so, you're happy now?" I said, for lack of anything better to say.

"No, I'm not happy," he said, suddenly acting all sad. Then he laughed and jumped up out of his chair. "I'm EC-STATIC! All the cool stuff I get to do! And everybody here loves it. They love *everything* I do. You should see their faces when I open a new store or put on a new play or release a new song or write a new book. You'd think I was some sort of god or something."

"It's a good thing they speak English." I knew I was opening up a can of worms with that one but figured I might as well try to get inside Mr. Arthur's head as best I could, since I was either going to be spending a lot of time with the guy or living in his dungeon.

"Well, they didn't used to," he said with a chuckle. "When I first arrived here I couldn't understand a thing anybody said. They all spoke different languages and, quite frankly, I don't think any of them understood what the others were saying. It all sounded like a bunch of gibberish, anyway. So I took it upon myself to teach them English."

"How did you do that?" I asked, overwhelmed at the thought of what a huge task that would be.

"I'm an English teacher!" he said with a laugh. "That's what I do! Hey, what do you have in your backpack? Anything fun?"

He jumped up out of his chair and headed over to me. I had taken my backpack off when I sat down and it was sitting next to my chair. I reached out to grab it but before I could, Mr. Arthur took it, unzipped it, and reached inside. The first thing he pulled out was my math book.

"*Introduction to Geometry, Twelfth Edition?* Man, they're still using that? What a bunch of cheapskates. You'd be better off if you had been born one township over, Iggy. The

Warner school system is way better than ours." He flipped through the book for a second. "Okay if I hang onto this? There's a few things I need to brush up on for my airplane."

I sort of shrugged my shoulders, not knowing what to say, since a big part of me just wanted to yell at him to get his hands out of my bag. I mean, he didn't know if I had anything embarrassing in there or not. For all he knew, I could have had a bunch of old underwear and a girl's coloring book hidden inside. Unfortunately, I knew I had something in there that was probably going to be much more valuable to him.

Mr. Arthur pulled out my dad's Shakespeare book and suddenly looked like his head was going to explode. He stared at it like it was a bag of diamonds and his mouth sort of opened and closed like a fish as he flipped slowly through its pages. His eyes looked like they were going to bug out of his head and I could hear Karen's voice in my brain saying, "Way to go, Iggy, you dope."

"I can't believe it," Mr. Arthur said as he got what looked like tears in his eyes. "I've spent every day since I've been here wishing I had this. I've tried to remember all the plays and the dialogue but I couldn't. The only one I could remember in any detail was *Hamlet* and even that never sounded right when we were rehearsing it. Why do you have this?"

"It's my dad's," I said, thinking maybe that would make him give it back to me. "I brought it to school for a class project. It's a really expensive book. He'll kill me if anything happens to it."

"Yeah, like you're ever going to see him again," he said with a snort as he flipped through the book again. Sensing that I was now staring at him like he had just told me he was going to kill me, which it sort of sounded like he did, he looked at me and got a worried look. "No, I don't mean anything's going to happen to you. I just mean, there's no way you're going to get back to our frequency, that's all."

Somehow, that didn't make me feel any better.

# 28

## MY DINNER WITH CHESTER

Mr. Arthur's dining room was huge.

I mean, huge like in those old black-and-white movies you see about super rich people who have a really long table and they sit at either end of it so that when somebody asks the other person to pass the salt, they have to yell, and then the butler has to get it from one person and walk it all the way down to the person at the other end. Well, this dining room made those rooms look small, and this table made those tables look like little ironing boards.

The table was as long as a basketball court and the room was as big as a gymnasium. Fortunately, Mr. Arthur didn't make us sit at the far ends of the table, because if he had, we would have had to yell our conversation using megaphones just so we could hear each other. But the fact that we were now sitting across from each other in the center of the table sort of made it feel like we were about to eat dinner off the top of the Great Wall of China. In fact, when we came into the dining room and he gestured for me to take a seat on the other side of the table, it took me about five minutes to walk all the way around to sit at my place.

As we sat there in silence, Mr. Arthur was flipping through the Shakespeare book, completely engrossed in it and looking, as my grandma used to say, "as giddy as a schoolgirl." Every time he'd get to a new play, he would give this little squeak of excitement, like he had forgotten that it existed. Clearly he was out of his head happy about all the new famous plays he could pass off as his own.

"Oh, they're going to love this one," he would say, then flip a few pages and say it again, like he hadn't just said it a few seconds earlier.

It wasn't until the feels who were his butlers and maids started bringing all the food out that I realized just how hungry I was. In fact, hungry's not really the right word. I was starving. Literally. I don't think I'd had anything to eat the entire time I'd been in this frequency because everything had been so weird and busy and nerve-racking from the second my rocket blew up, which had sort of made me forget about food for a while.

The main butler feel, as well as a bunch of other female feels dressed like French maids, brought out platters and dishes and bowls and baskets filled with stuff that all sort of looked like the food we had back home. They even brought out what looked like a Thanksgiving turkey on a big silver tray. It wasn't until they carved into it that I could tell this was no turkey, since the meat was all purple and had stripes of yellow running through it. As hungry as I was, the minute I saw the color of that meat I sort of felt like throwing up. Except that there was nothing in my stomach to barf up.

"Dig in!" said Mr. Arthur as he started grabbing bowls and spooning tons of food onto his plate. I reached out and grabbed what looked like a bowl of corn. I scooped a big pile of it onto my plate since I really like corn. ("Yeah, because it's mostly sugar," my dad used to say. "Corn is the candy of the vegetable world!" was his other favorite saying, meaning that even when I thought I was eating healthy, I wasn't eating healthy.) I took a whiff of the corn, since I always smell stuff before I eat it, a habit I got into after Frank Gutenkunitz hid a cat turd under my green beans in the cafeteria one day, and it was a good thing I did, because the corn smelled really bad. It didn't even smell like corn, except maybe corn that had been sitting in the trash for a couple of days.

I didn't want to insult Mr. Arthur and so just figured that maybe this one dish was a mistake. I grabbed another bowl that was filled with mashed potatoes. I smacked a glob of it onto my plate and then secretly put my nose down over it. The potatoes also smelled bad, sort of like dirty socks.

"You're not going to like anything if you keep smelling it first," said Mr. Arthur, which almost made me jump out of my skin because I thought he wasn't watching me. "Everything's different here and, even though I've been working on an additive to make their food taste like ours, it still isn't perfected. But I did get them to make the food *look* like our food back home. So even though it looks familiar, none of it is going to taste the way you're used to it tasting, which is probably throwing you. But it's good. Try it with an open mind."

It was pretty embarrassing getting caught smelling all my food. And, since I was hungrier than I was grossed out at that moment, I figured I'd better get something in my stomach, no matter how stinky it was.

I took a few kernels of "corn" on my fork and put them in my mouth. Since I didn't really know what it was supposed to taste like but since I was also expecting it to taste terrible, it actually wasn't bad at all. It kinda tasted like cheddar cheese. I had to figure that the reason it smelled so bad when I took my first whiff was because I was expecting it to smell exactly like corn. It was like the time I asked my mom to pour me a Coke but she didn't want me to have a Coke and so she filled my tumbler with milk and since the tumbler was made out of plastic that you couldn't see through and since I was looking at the TV instead of what I was about to drink, I took a huge gulp of it and spit it out all over the table because it tasted so bad. I mean, I liked milk a lot and the milk in the tumbler wasn't sour or anything, but my taste buds and I were expecting Coke. When your mouth is ready for one taste and it gets the complete opposite, then even something like chocolate cake can taste bad if you were expecting it to be spaghetti.

"See? I told you so," said Mr. Arthur with a laugh. "Just keep an open mind and you're really going to enjoy this meal."

I ate some potatoes and they tasted like chicken and I ate some grapes and they tasted like onions and I had some French fries and they tasted like oranges. It was almost like some kind of game, trying to guess what each food item would taste like, sort of like when you grab a chocolate out of one of those assortment boxes and you have no idea what's inside it. But with those, you know that at least you'll have the taste of chocolate to save you if what's inside is sort of gross.

The food was doing its job. I was getting full and was also feeling a lot better. You never really know how bad you feel when you're hungry until you finally eat. Then you suddenly realize that if you were in a bad mood or were feeling jumpy or grouchy or dizzy, it's because your stomach was empty. Well, as my stomach was filling up, I was starting to feel a bit more like my old self. The only difference was my old self was still living in a new and strange world run by a dictator who used to be an English teacher.

"So, Iggy," Mr. Arthur said as he chewed on a mouthful of the purple and yellow "turkey" meat. "How much stuff do you know?"

"Excuse me?" I said, confused and with my mouth full of peas that tasted like Salisbury steak.

"What things do you know by heart? What songs? Movies? Books? Anything you can write down that we can put out?" He was staring at me as he tried to cut a particularly tough piece of the purple turkey meat on his plate.

"Um . . . I don't know. Not much. I've never really been good at memorizing things." Man, that meat looked weird.

"Well," he said as he struggled with his knife, "I'm sure you'll start to remember lots of stuff once you settle in here."

"Yeah, I guess so," I said as my mind tried to figure out what he meant by the phrase "settle in here."

"I'm telling you, man, I'm so happy about that Shakespeare book. I think I might even close down my *Hamlet* just so that I can fix the things I forgot. Did you get to see my production of it?"

I looked at him, surprised, to see if he was joking. He didn't seem to be.

"Uh . . . no. I was too busy trying not to get killed by your army." I didn't say it in a mean way. It just sort of came out of my mouth because it was true.

"Oh, yeah, sorry about that," he said as he put the tough piece of purple meat into his mouth. "They weren't really trying to kill you, though. They were just trying to get Karen."

"Are they trying to kill Karen?" I asked, sounding a bit more freaked out than I intended.

"No," he said with a laugh as he chewed. "They're just trying to catch her to bring her back here."

"Really? 'Cause they sort of seemed like they were trying to kill her, since they were swinging swords and axes and throwing knives at her." I suddenly couldn't stop saying things that I knew might possibly make him mad. Fortunately, he just kept chewing and acting like we were having a really normal conversation.

"They know she's a fighter and so they were trying not to get killed themselves, probably. She's one scary girl."

I nodded, since it was sort of hard to argue with that statement. I ate another spoonful of the cheddar cheese–tasting corn and tried to figure out if I should say what I knew I was about to say.

"Why are you so worried about Karen being out there?"

"I'm not," he said with a laugh.

"Then why are you trying to catch her?"

He stared at me for a few seconds as he chewed, then he set down his fork and knife on his plate.

*Click.*

"Look," he said seriously, "Karen says a lot of bad things about me. And it's not that my ego can't take it. I'm fine with criticism. But I'm the *President*. And I can't have her out there spreading lies about me."

"Lies?"

"Yeah, you know. You hung with her. She says stupid things like I'm dangerous and that I'm oppressing everybody and that I'm a dictator and all. Look, you're hanging with me," he said, leaning forward and pointing at himself like he was trying to prove a point. "I'm not a dictator. I'm a nice guy, right?"

I didn't know what to say. Insecure or not, the guy *was* a dictator. I just knew that if I made him mad and he locked me in prison then there would be nothing I could do to help myself get out of here and back to Karen. Assuming she was still okay.

"Uh . . . yeah," was what I finally stammered out, feeling like I had just betrayed Foo and all her people. Fortunately, I guess he was so certain that I was going to agree with him that apparently my unenthusiastic affirmation of his niceness sounded like a ringing endorsement to him.

"Yeah!" he said with a happy laugh. "I'm a nice guy! Let's have some dessert."

* * *

After we ate what looked like Ding Dongs but which were ill-advisedly called Art Dongs and which tasted more like broccoli than chocolate, Mr. Arthur said he had something else he wanted to show me. We left the dining room and went up a long staircase that led to a door. Mr. Arthur opened the door and we stepped out onto the roof of the White House. There were a couple of gorilla guards up there and they immediately bowed when they saw their president.

"You can leave us," Mr. Arthur said to them politely.

They both bowed again and then again and then backed out through the doorway, never turning away from Mr. Arthur. ***Boom! Crash! Thump thump thump!*** One of them fell backward down the stairs as the other one kept bowing and quickly closed the door. This army needs some backing-up lessons, I thought to myself.

Mr. Arthur shook his head and chuckled, then led me over to the edge of the roof.

"Check this out," he said with a smile that showed he was sure I was about to be impressed.

We got to the edge and I saw the bizarre city of Lester-ville stretching out before me. I looked up at Mr. Arthur and saw him staring at it like it he was a proud father staring at his newborn baby.

"It's beautiful, isn't it?" he asked me with what looked like the beginning of tears in his eyes.

I stared at it. It was a city, all right. And it was filled with lots of stuff that he had made, even though it was all based on stuff from our frequency. But as for the adjective "beautiful," well, that was sort of, as they say, in the eye of the beholder. His eye beheld beauty. My eye beheld something that looked like it was about to fall apart if someone sneezed on it.

"I worked so hard to make that," he said as if he were talking to himself more than to me. "When I found this place it was so primitive. All the creatures who lived here seemed so unhappy. They were just going about their business, living their lives, not having anything to wear, not living in buildings that looked nice, not having any entertainment, not enjoying all the things we take for granted back in our frequency.

"They couldn't even communicate with each other. It was all just a lot of grunts and chirps and howls and squeaks and none of it made any sense. I could tell they were just miserable. And I ought to know, because *I* was miserable. I knew I was stuck in this place and I couldn't understand what anybody was saying and so I knew I had to make it better for everyone. And I did."

"How did you do it all?" I asked, truly curious since I had no idea how one person could have changed so much stuff.

"Hey, like I said, I'm a teacher," he said with a smile. "I taught them. I rolled up my sleeves and got to know them and just went one step at a time. I started to teach them English by telling them the words for different objects, then once they caught on to that I taught them how to form sentences. More and more of them got interested in learning and pretty soon, lots of them were speaking and we could communicate. And then those creatures went out and persuaded more creatures to come and learn English and soon it seemed like the whole place could speak and understand. And then once we could do that, the world was an open book. I could teach them music, I could write them plays and teach them to act and everybody else could watch and enjoy. I could show them how to build buildings and make clothes and help them to do all the things that I knew were going to make their lives a thousand times better. And I did. And there it is."

He held his hand out to the city and smiled again.

"You did all that in *five years*?" I asked, amazed at the thought of Mr. Arthur working that hard just so everybody could understand him.

"Hey, what *else* did I have to do?" He laughed.

"And you got them to build the whole city that fast?"

"Once they got a taste of our world, they couldn't get enough of it. I showed them some drawings of buildings I had sketched and they wanted to make some of their own. They all pitched in and got to work and suddenly buildings were popping up all over the place. Granted, their work wasn't perfect but the fact that they were doing it made it all seem so . . . wonderful.

"I mean, I even think it all looks better than it did back home. More creative, you know? Anyway, I drew up the plans for Art's Square and the next thing I knew that was being built, too. And then I showed them my design for the White House here and pretty soon that was done. It was amazing."

"Why's the town called Lesterville?"

"Lester is my middle name."

"But why didn't you call it Arthurville or Artville?"

He looked at me and chuckled. "Iggy, I don't want people to think I have a big ego."

Uh . . . no comment.

"So how'd you get an army?" I asked this because I really was curious. I didn't think it would be something he might get weird about.

Mr. Arthur gave me a disapproving look. "They're not an army, Iggy. They're just sort of my police force. Sadly, every large group of people needs a few of their peers to make sure they don't do things they shouldn't do. It's like having hall monitors in school, you know? If no one was watching what went on in the hallways, anything could happen. People could do things they shouldn't do and disrupt other classes or not participate in the things they should be involved in. So I'm just having the creatures who like me and like the city I've created here help out by keeping an eye on their friends, that's all."

He gave me a fatherly smile and a pat on the back that sort of indicated he didn't want to talk about this anymore. I desperately wanted to ask him why he had his "police force" destroy the flying people's city but got the feeling that if I brought it up he might get mad. And I wasn't really in the mood to get thrown in that dungeon that Karen had told me about.

"C'mon, let's go and pick you out a room to stay in," he said as he headed back to the door. As I turned and hoped that he was talking about a real room with a bed and carpeting and a bathroom and not some hideous concrete cell in which I'd have to pee and poo into a bucket, I looked up and noticed that high above in the sky, Foo was hovering and watching me.

Mr. Arthur turned and looked at me from the doorway. I snapped my eyes down from the sky to meet his eyes, not wanting him to look up and see Foo.

"You coming, Ignatius MacFarland?"

"Yes, sir," I said, trying not to sound caught.

"Iggy, my dad was 'sir.' You can call me Chester," he said with a laugh.

"Yes, sir . . . uh, Chester," I said as I walked through the door. I glanced up quickly and saw Foo fly away. As I headed down the stairs to select my new room, I couldn't help but wonder and worry about where Karen and Foo and all the flying people were going to sleep that night.

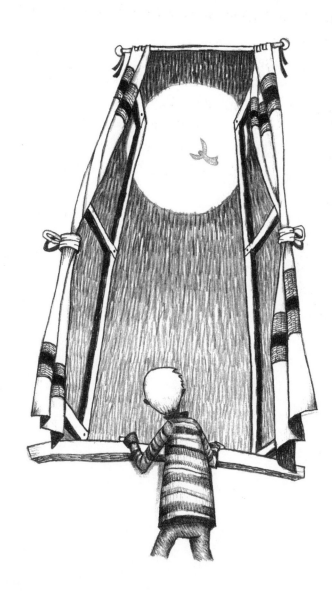

## 29

# BEHIND THE GREEN DOOR

As I lay in the really soft and comfortable bed in the big bedroom that Mr. Arthur told me I could have as my own private place for as long as I stayed there, I started to get really depressed. It had been kind of nice and exciting being away from home in this weird new world, and when I was running around and fighting with Karen and seeing all sorts of new things for the first time my mind was too busy to realize that I might never see my parents or my friends or my hometown again. I had always wanted to leave the Earth and imagined that the relief of not having Frank Gutenkunitz trying to beat me up and humiliate me every day would make me immune to any kind of homesickness.

However, now that I was sitting in bed in a room that only had grandma furniture in it and a huge painting of Mr. Arthur staring at me from the opposite wall, and with only my schoolbooks to keep me company (and not even my dad's Shakespeare book, which Mr. Arthur had taken with him), I suddenly got really really sad. What if I had to stay here for the rest of my life? What would I do? Help Mr. Arthur keep passing off things from our world as inventions he thought up? What was he going to do to Karen when he finally found her? And was I ever going to see her or Foo or the cat who thought it was a dog again?

Just as my brain was starting to get that spinning feeling it does when things become overwhelming and I think I'm going to have a panic attack, like when I have a big paper due in class the next day that I haven't even started to write yet, I heard a weird noise outside my room.

*. . . clank . . . clank . . .*

It was far away but just loud enough to snap me out of my self-pity. Normally if I was at home watching TV or playing video games or working on my computer, it was the kind of noise I wouldn't even have paid attention to. But since I was sitting in a room by myself with absolutely nothing to do except be depressed, I decided to see what it was. I got out of bed and went to the door. I was wearing a pair of pajamas Mr. Arthur had given me that read SLEEPIN' ON ARTHUR TIME! with a picture of him giving a big thumbs-up across the front. I had no idea what it meant but had to figure it was something he thought was cool, like when my dad would hear a rapper use some slang term and then blurt it out at dinner to show us that he wasn't as old and uncool as we all knew he really was.

I put my ear against the door and listened.

*. . . clank . . . clank . . .*

I slipped on my shoes, opened the door, and stepped out into the hallway. It was dark except for some light from Lesterville coming in through a window at the end of the hallway. I walked quietly down the hall, not wanting to wake anybody up, even though I had no idea if there was anybody around *to* wake up.

*. . . clank . . . clank . . .*

The sound was getting louder as I headed for the end of the hallway. I kept looking nervously behind me, just in case the butler or some army guys were sneaking up on me while I was busy sneaking up on the clanking sound. The floor kept creaking loudly and I realized that the White House was basically as poorly built as everything else in Lesterville, even though it looked nicer. *Creak.* I'd stop and hold my breath, then take a few more steps. *Creak.* Man, this place was annoying.

*. . . clank . . . clank . . .*

I finally got to the end of the hallway and saw a green door. There was light coming out from the small space between the bottom of it and the carpet. I put my ear against the door and listened.

*Clank. Clank.*

Whatever was clanking was clanking behind that door. I carefully put my hand on the knob and gave it a small, slow turn to see if it was unlocked. It was. Should I crack open the door and take a look? I asked myself. Why the heck not? I've got nothing else to do.

I very slowly and cautiously started to push the door open, trying to crack it just enough for me to peek through. I put my eye to the gap and squinted against the bright lights inside the room. As my eye began to adjust and come into focus, I saw something very strange indeed.

The room was sort of a big, dirty warehouse with lots of Mr. Arthur's junk piled around. It looked like it was one of his workshops but that it had been taken over for another purpose. All his inventions and materials were pushed up against the walls and a big open area was in the middle of the floor.

A weird futuristic machine that looked a little bit like a really big version of those metal detector security things you walk through at the airport was in the center of the floor. It was sort of like a giant archway with a really high-tech computer screen on one side. Mr. Arthur was standing next to the screen talking to someone I couldn't see because they

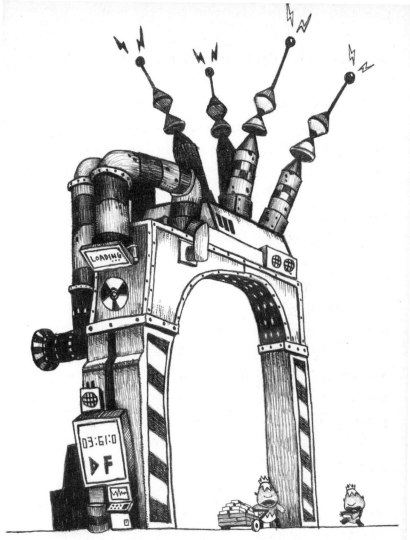

were blocked by the machine. And then I saw the source of all the clanking — two giant purple babies were stacking up a big pile of gold bars underneath the machine's archway. They were just like the gold bars I'd seen in movies about bank robberies and the U.S. mint, all shiny and rectangular and heavy-looking. The babies were taking bars one at a time off a large cart with big wheels that had a lot more of the bars piled up on it. Standing behind them was a very mean-looking gorilla guard who kept growling at them and holding out his sword to let them know that if they stopped unloading the gold he would do something terrible to them.

And then I saw that there were more gold bars piled up on the right side of the room. I don't know how much gold bars are actually worth but I'm confident enough to say that the amount of bars in that place was worth a buttload of money back in our frequency.

"Why would they destroy the entire city?" I heard Mr. Arthur saying in a kind of panicky voice to whomever he was talking to. "It doesn't make any sense."

"You really are an idiot, aren't you, Arthur?"

It was a man's voice, the voice of someone who was used to speaking English. It didn't have any of the uncertainty and weird pronunciations that all the creatures in this frequency had. It almost sounded like someone from *our* frequency.

"I just told them to go and find the girl and the newcomer," said Mr. Arthur in the same tone I used to use to get out of trouble with my teachers when I was late with my homework. "I didn't tell them to destroy the entire place."

And it was then that I saw whom he was talking to. A man, slightly older and about two feet shorter than Mr. Arthur, who was wearing a suit and tie on his rather pudgy body, stepped out from behind the machine and got in Mr. Arthur's face. The man was angry but not yelling. He was what my father would call intense.

"You've really complicated things, Arthur," said the man in the tie. "This operation was almost complete. All I had to do was cart the rest of the gold from the mines to here. We were working in an area where the flyers never went. Our transportation path was completely unobserved. And so what do you do? You destroy their city and fill the sky with them!"

"But I didn't tell my guys to destroy the city!"

"The groundies hate the flyers! Everybody knows that! Don't you ever get out of this ridiculous White House and talk to anybody? Or are you just too busy ripping off everybody with actual talent from our frequency?"

Mr. Arthur stood there, not quite knowing what to say. The man in the tie sighed, then looked over at the gold.

"It doesn't matter," said the man. "I'll finish this operation and get out of here and then you can do whatever you want with this place. You can be Shakespeare and Frank Sinatra and Leonardo da Vinci and anyone else you want to be. But for now you have to make sure that nothing impedes the transport of the gold out of this frequency, do you understand me? If anything goes wrong I'm holding you personally responsible and will effectively *end* your presidency. You got it?"

As Mr. Arthur just stood there and nodded, clearly afraid of the guy in the tie, I stared at the weird machine that the gold was being put inside. Transport the gold out of this frequency? I couldn't believe it. That machine was able to go back and forth between this world and ours. And the guy in the tie was using it to steal gold. How long had he been here? Karen had lived in the White House when she first arrived and yet she had never mentioned anybody from our frequency other than Mr. Arthur. Who was this guy?

"What are you going to do with the newcomer?" the guy in the tie asked as he turned and started counting the gold bars.

I stiffened a bit at the mention of myself. It was one of those moments when you both want to hear what somebody is going to say about you and yet you sort of wish you weren't there because since the person thinks they're talking privately about you they might say something really mean or embarrassing. But I listened because I figured it was probably pretty important that I know what he was saying about me.

"I've got the newcomer under control," said Mr. Arthur with a "don't worry" tone in his voice. "He seems like a smart kid and I'll just keep him here with me. I need some-one I trust to help me with the day-to-day running of this place and I think that he's very trainable. I mean, he really likes me and is very impressed with everything I've done so far."

I had to marvel at Mr. Arthur's ego. Even though I hadn't said anything too negative to him, I certainly hadn't ever acted like I was that impressed with what he was doing, nor had I done anything to make him think that I really liked him. But I guess people hear what they want to hear.

"Well, if I were you, I'd keep him locked up until we're finished and I've gotten all the gold out of here. Because if he causes any trouble whatsoever, I'll neutralize him myself."

And upon hearing that, I quickly and quietly closed the door and ran silently back to my room. I'd seen enough TV shows and movies to know that *neutralize* was just a fancy, less-scary-sounding word for *kill*. And I wasn't looking to get killed.

I got back in my room and sat on the edge of my bed. Af-ter all of Mr. Arthur's talk about improving the place and making the creatures' lives better, was his entire plan to simply steal gold from this frequency? But the man in the tie said that he was going to leave with the gold and then Mr. Arthur could do what he wanted. It was all really con-fusing, and I didn't know what to do. Should I try to get in the machine and go back home? Should I escape and find Karen? Could Foo help me? Did she hate me now because she thought I was friends with Mr. Arthur? And could I even get out of here?

There were no guards in the hallway but there had to be others around and now I knew that if I got caught doing anything, the man in the tie was going to kill me. I tried to imagine what Karen would do if she was in this situation but I knew the answer and it didn't seem like something I was capable of doing. I could hear her telling me to stop being a wuss and get up and get out of there, even if I had to fight off an army and kick Mr. Arthur in the nuts.

Man, how I wished I was Karen at that moment.

I heard a tapping on my window and nearly jumped out of my skin. I turned quickly and saw Foo hovering outside. I got up and went to the window and tried to open it, but it was locked. I didn't want to yell to her through the window because I knew someone would hear me and I didn't want to take a chance of getting either myself or Foo in trouble. And so I just gave her a lame little wave hello.

She pointed at me and made a face that said, "Are you all right?"

I nodded and gave her a "What are you doing?" look.

She smiled at me and mouthed, "I'm checking on you."

"How are *you?*" I mouthed back, since I had merely been captured while she had seen her entire city destroyed that very day.

She smiled again and nodded, which I guessed meant she was all right. She then put her hand on the glass and gave me a look that said, "Everything is going to be okay." My heart felt like somebody had just filled it full of helium and before I even knew what I was doing, I reached out my hand and put it up on the glass against hers. I smiled at her since I suddenly realized just how happy I was to see her. Even though I'd only known her for about twenty-four hours, and even though she was a person from another frequency who could fly, I really really really liked her. And I knew that she liked me back.

Foo moved in closer to the glass and raised her other hand. I thought she was going to put that on the glass, too, and so I began to raise my other hand to meet hers. However, all she did was give me a friendly shake of her head and point to something behind me. Before I could turn around to look, a hand clamped down hard on my shoulder.

"YEEEAAAGGG!!!" I screamed as my heart leaped into my throat.

I spun around and was face-to-face with Karen.

"C'mon, lover boy," she said like she wanted to laugh at me. "Let's get out of here."

"How did you get in?!" I whispered loudly, my heart pounding out of my chest from the rush of adrenaline she had just given me. "Weren't there guards all over the place?"

"Yeah," she said with a shrug.

And then I heard the sound of tons of guards running through the hallway toward my room.

"Oh, man," I said as my stomach fell into my shoes. "You just never make stuff easy, do you?"

"What fun would that be?" she said with a smile as I saw the glint of swords and battle-axes appear outside my door.

# 30

# NOW WE'RE IN TROUBLE

Karen reached over her shoulders with both hands and pulled two gorilla guard swords out of the back of a woven battle vest she had made from heavy rope. She tossed one of the swords at me handle-first. I caught it before my brain even realized that my hand had been smart enough to reach out for it.

"Try to do a better job than you did in the forest," she said as the gorilla guards ran into the room.

Oh, great, I thought. Nothing like heading into battle wearing pajamas.

Karen gave a yell and ran at the guards, swinging her sword in a figure-eight pattern that made it impossible for them to hit her with their weapons. The guards all looked startled at the power of her attack but quickly had to react as she charged toward them. They stuck out their swords. **_CLANG! CLANG!_** She swung her weapon into theirs so hard that the guards all spun sideways as the swords flew out of their hands.

"Let's go!" she yelled as she grabbed my shirt collar and dashed for the door, practically pulling me off my feet. I snatched my backpack and clothes off the chair next to the door, then raised my sword and pointed it rather lamely at the guards as we ran past them, hoping they would think I was as tough as Karen was. But their faces just filled with anger as they grabbed their swords and ran after us into the hallway.

As we sprinted toward the stairs with the gorilla guards running after us, I heard the green door behind us open. I looked back and saw Mr. Arthur emerge.

"It's the Anti-Art!" Mr. Arthur yelled. "GET THEM!!!"

We tried to run down the stairs quickly without falling and killing ourselves. Running down stairs is hard enough but it's even worse when you're carrying a big sword and getting chased by creatures who want to chop your head off. The guards were hopping down the stairs after us but luckily their feet were so big they were having trouble keeping their footing.

We ran down the curving staircase into the lobby and saw the front door. Suddenly, the door flew open and the huge mole commander and several gorilla guards appeared, weapons drawn.

"Well, well, well," said the mole commander with what I assumed was a smile. "If it isn't my old friends. You two just keep making it easy for us, don't you?"

"Yeah," said Karen with a sarcastic laugh. "You really did a great job catching me last time."

"Oh, we just let you go," he said with his own version of a sarcastic laugh. "We were after your friend there. If we'd really wanted you, we would have gotten you."

"Yeah?" Karen said as she raised her sword at him. "Do you want me now?"

The mole commander and the gorilla guards behind him all raised their weapons threateningly.

"Oh, yes," said the mole commander. "We do." He then stepped forward and turned his blade so that the light glinted off it onto Karen's face. "Nice knowing you."

And with that, he took a huge swing at both of us that showed he really did intend to detach our heads from our bodies. We both dropped to the floor, the ax literally clipping off the top inch of my hair.

"Don't kill the boy!" I heard Mr. Arthur yell from the stairs as all the gorilla guards ran toward us.

"Looks like someone made himself a friend," Karen said to me with a scowl. "Well, guess what? You're my ticket out of here now."

And before I even had a chance to process what she said, she threw her arm around my chest, stood up quickly, and pulled my back tight against her, turning me into a human shield as my sword dropped out of my startled hand and thumped onto the carpet. Then she put her sword up under my chin and turned to face the approaching guards.

"One more step and I cut off his head," she yelled at them.

The guards all stopped and looked up at Mr. Arthur. He put out his hand, signaling them to wait. Then he looked at Karen and made a frustrated face.

"She's bluffing," said a voice.

We all looked up at the top of the stairs and I saw the man in the tie come around the corner. He came down a few steps and looked at Karen and me.

"You're not really going to fall for that old gag, are you, Mr. President?" the man in the tie said with a smile.

"Who the hell are you?" said Karen, sounding very surprised to see another person from our dimension.

"The name's Golonski," the man said coolly. "Herbert Golonski."

Karen burst out laughing, then said, "You're joking, right?"

"It's not nice to make fun of people's names, Miss," said the man, looking a bit perturbed.

"He's right, you know," I added quietly. "I hate when people laugh at my na —"

"Shut up," she growled into my ear.

"Karen," said Mr. Arthur, "just let Iggy go. I'm not looking to hurt you."

"Huh. Really? And exactly how does the phrase 'Don't kill the boy' fit into that?" she said about as sarcastically as anything I'd ever heard anyone say.

"Why wouldn't he want to kill you?" asked the man we now knew as Herbert Golonski. "You've been trying to subvert his presidency and destroy this city. Where we come from, that's called treason."

"Gee, I thought where we came from it was called liberating an oppressed people from a dictatorship."

"Hey, I'm not a dictator," said Mr. Arthur, sounding highly insulted. "I've done nothing but nice things for the people of this city."

"Yeah, and if they didn't agree with you or want what you were giving them they were just free to do whatever they wanted, right?" she said to Mr. Arthur as she slowly backed the two of us away from the guards.

"Mr. President, you don't have to listen to any of this," said Herbert with a shake of his head. "She's not going to kill the boy." He then looked at the mole commander and got a very angry look. "Grab her!"

The mole commander nodded and then gestured angrily to the gorilla guards. "You heard the man. Grab her!"

The gorilla guards all started to stalk forward as Karen continued to back up. Since we weren't moving toward the door and seemed to be backing into a corner, I had no idea what Karen was going to do. I felt her sword press harder into my neck.

"Uh . . . Karen," I said as delicately as I could, "are you really going to kill me?"

"Yes," she said in a scary tone. "As soon as we get away from these wackos."

And with that, she suddenly flung the two of us backward, holding on to me tightly.

*CRASH!*

We smashed through the window. The next thing I knew we were flipping through the air as shattering glass fell all around us.

"Brace yourself!" she yelled as we twisted in the air. Since we were on the first floor, I knew that we were going to hit the ground quickly and so put my hands up to make sure that I didn't land directly on my head and break my neck. She let go of me and did the same.

*WHAM!* The two of us hit the ground hard, landing painfully on our shoulders. I felt a shower of glass fall onto me and put my hands up to block it from cutting my face. Fortunately, the glass in this frequency was a lot more like brittle rock candy than the dangerous glass we have back home and so it bounced off our faces and hands like pieces of plastic.

Before we could even recover from hitting the ground, we heard the sound of the guards running out the door.

"Run!" Karen yelled as she jumped up. I shoved my clothes into my backpack and sprinted after her in my *Sleepin' on Arthur Time!* pajamas across the White House lawn.

I looked ahead and saw that a bunch of army guys and White House guards, as well as the giant baby in the tie, were blocking the front gate, their weapons drawn.

"Where do we run *to?*" I yelled at her in a panic.

"Just follow me," she yelled back over her shoulder as she veered and sped toward the high fence surrounding the yard. "And don't twist your ankle or run out of steam because if you do, this time I'm not coming back for you."

She leaped and landed halfway up the fence, grabbing the bars while still holding her sword, and quickly used her hands and feet to scramble up it like a monkey. I jumped onto the fence and tried the same thing but my now famous lack of upper body strength suddenly found me just hanging on as my feet tried to get a grip on the bars. Karen was already on the top of the fence and squeezing between the spikes when she looked down and saw me.

"Climb, you lame-o!" she yelled as I looked back and saw that the gorilla guards were almost at the fence. "Use your feet!"

My shoes finally got a grip on the bars and I scrambled higher up the fence, which was good because suddenly there was a huge *CLANG!* I looked down to see that one of the guards had thrown an ax at my legs and had just missed me.

"Hey, I thought they weren't supposed to kill me!" I shouted as I tried not to freak out.

"Yeah, but he didn't say anything about not cutting off your legs," said Karen as she jumped down to the ground outside the White House yard. "That's just the kind of guy Arthur is."

Not wanting to lose any of my limbs, I pulled myself up as hard as I could and flung myself into the air. "Oh, man!" was all I heard Karen say as I flew over the fence completely out of control, my arms and legs flailing all over the place like a flying squirrel that suddenly realized it couldn't fly.

*WHAM!* I slammed into the ground face-first as my arms and legs smashed down awkwardly.

*CLANG-CLANG-CLANG!* I looked over and saw all the guards hit the fence, their swords and axes banging against the bars, then saw them start to scramble up using their weird three legs and feet-hands in a way that showed they were pretty good at climbing things.

"Oh, God, C'MON!" yelled Karen as she grabbed my

shirt again and pulled me up. Fortunately I didn't seem to have any bones that were broken, although even if I had I think I was too scared to feel anything.

Karen and I sprinted down the road and into the city as more and more of Mr. Arthur's army ran out of the White House yard after us.

Man, for a guy who had consistently flunked gym class, I was now doing an awful lot of physical activity.

We flew down the road as I heard the pounding feet of the gorillas behind us. They were our main concern at the moment, since they were one of the few creatures in this frequency that had any speed on the ground. Unfortunately, Mr. Arthur's army seemed to have an endless supply of them. I looked back and saw a few of the giant babies chugging along behind the gorillas but they looked like sumo wrestlers who were about five seconds away from having massive heart attacks.

It wasn't until we ran through the first intersection that I realized the gorilla guards weren't the only army members who were going to cause us problems. Coming down both streets on either side of us were two large groups of the giant rolling potato bug creatures and the four-legged octopus things with the fly-heads. They all seemed to have even more speed than the gorillas, with the potato bugs rolling like speeding tires and the octopuses galloping like some kind of creepy noodle-legged horses.

I could hear the loud metal clicking of the spiked weapons the octopuses had on their feet, which sounded like an enormous stampede of huge dogs whose nails hadn't been clipped in years. The potato bug guys were all twirling their wagon wheel blades and glaring at us with their tentacle eyes. We zoomed through the intersection and, a few seconds later, the potato bugs and octopuses merged with the gorilla guards and continued to chase us, their weapons ready to do whatever damage to us they darn well pleased.

Karen looked over her shoulder and saw the huge army of creatures that was now hot on our tails.

"We're not gonna outrun them," she yelled, then looked forward for some sort of escape idea. She saw the theater where *Hamlet* was playing up ahead. "Iggy! In here!"

Karen sprinted over to the theater door, where a feel was dressed like an usher, and pushed it open with a bang.

"Hey, where's your ticket?" yelled the feel as Karen and I ran past him. I saw him look back just in time to see the horde of army guys running at him. "Oh, no!" was all I heard him say as the gorillas and potato bugs crashed into the doors of the theater, knocking them off their cheap hinges and sending the usher flying.

Karen and I ran through the lobby and then through a second set of doors into the theater. We slammed them shut and Karen slid her sword through the handles to keep the doors from opening.

"That'll hold them for about three seconds," Karen said with a snort.

"Shhh!" we heard someone say behind us.

We turned and saw that the play was in midperformance. The audience in the large, dark theater was filled with creatures, and onstage was a one-eyed extendable weasel guy who was dressed in tights and wearing an outfit that looked vaguely like a costume you would see someone wearing in a real Shakespeare play. He was talking super loud, way louder than you're really supposed to talk when you're in a play even though you have to talk loud enough so that the people in the back of the theater can hear you.

"To be or not to be, that is the questio —"

**BOOM!** The army of creatures all smashed against the door, which surprisingly withstood their first impact. The sword in the door handles buckled and bent but didn't give way. The weasel onstage stopped and looked at the back of the theater, completely confused and startled.

"Hey, shut up back there!" he said as he extended his body up to full height and put his hands on his hips. "I'm acting here."

The entire audience also turned to look, but by that point Karen and I were running up the main aisle.

We jumped on the stage as the weasel spun around trying to figure out who we were. Then he saw Karen and got a terrified look on his face.

"The Anti-Art!" he screamed in a high-pitched voice like a little girl.

**BOOM!** The army burst through the doors, sending splinters of wood everywhere. As the army guys swarmed through the theater and the audience screamed and ran for their lives, Karen and I bolted into the backstage area.

Karen looked around for a door but there wasn't one. "You've gotta be kidding me! He didn't even build a stage door?!"

We heard the sound of the army running through the theater and realized we had to do something quickly.

"Oh, man, I don't even have my freakin' sword!" said Karen angrily as she stared at the approaching armed creatures. Then she looked over at something. "Quick! We're going up!"

She ran over to a ladder that was bolted onto the back wall of the stage and started to climb it. I looked up and saw that it led to a catwalk high above. I had no idea what we were going to do once we got up there but since the alternative of just standing still and getting wiped out by hundreds of metal blades didn't seem very appealing, I ran to the ladder and followed her up.

The army guys all swarmed the stage and ran after us into the wings. Karen was already at the top of the ladder as I struggled to make the halfway point.

"Hurry!" she yelled down at me as she jumped onto the catwalk.

"Why?" I yelled back. "There's nowhere to go up there except back down."

"Wanna bet?" she said as she reached up and knocked her hand against the very tinny and cheap-sounding ceiling.

The ladder shook suddenly and I looked down to see gorilla guy after gorilla guy jumping onto it. The ladder started to moan from all the weight, and the bolts that were holding it on to the wall started to pull loose. This gave me the extra adrenaline rush I needed to get to the top.

As I jumped onto the catwalk, Karen pulled a metal pole out of a railing that had a rope tied to it. The rope unreeled off the catwalk like fishing line that had been cast into the middle of a stream and we heard the huge painted backdrop for the *Hamlet* play go crashing onto the stage, falling on top of the army creatures. They all started yelling and thrashing around under the huge piece of canvas as the gorillas on the ladder looked down, surprised. They then started climbing faster as the ladder continued to creak and more bolts started popping out of the wall.

*POONK!* Karen punched the metal pole through the ceiling. "Man, this place is such a piece of junk," she said as she started pulling down on the pole and cutting through the ceiling the same way you would open a can with one of those Swiss Army knife can openers.

Karen and I looked down and saw that the gorillas were almost up to the catwalk.

"Um, unless you want us to get killed, I'd do something about those guys," she said, nodding her head over at the guards as she continued to open a hole in the metal roof.

I ran over to the ladder just as the top gorilla was about to grab the catwalk. I kicked the top of the ladder to push it away from the wall. The good part was that it immediately broke loose and started to fall back into the theater. The bad part was that the top gorilla grabbed my pajama leg and held on as the ladder started to fall.

I was immediately yanked off my feet. I fell down face-first and grabbed on to the grated metal floor of the catwalk with my fingers to keep from getting pulled over the side. The ladder stopped with a jerk as the gorilla held on to my pajama bottoms, using me to keep the ladder from falling backward.

"He's got the leg of my pajamas!" I screamed.

"Then take them off!" Karen screamed back as she turned and saw my predicament.

"Are you out of your mind?!" I yelled back. I mean, an emergency was an emergency but it still didn't mean you had to show the world your underwear (which fortunately I was still wearing!).

Karen pulled the metal pole out of the ceiling and ran to me. She reached over the side of the catwalk and swung the pole down onto the gorilla's hand with all her might, just missing my leg.

The guard screamed and opened his hand in pain, causing the ladder to resume its fall backward.

"Nice work," Karen said as I pulled myself back up onto the catwalk and we watched the ladder crash down onto the stage and into the seats of the theater as gorilla guards tumbled painfully off of it. "That'll buy us some time."

Before I could thank her for saving me, we heard a ripping sound. We looked down at the stage and saw the octopus guys tear through the canvas and start climbing straight up the wall with their sucker feet.

"So much for time," said Karen as her eyes went wide. We both jumped up and ran to the hole in the ceiling. Karen grabbed a coil of rope off the catwalk, then jumped up and hoisted herself through the hole. I looked down and saw that the octopus guys were almost at the catwalk.

"Give me your hand!" Karen yelled at me as she held her arm down through the hole. I went to take her hand, which was cut from grabbing the jagged edge when she climbed up.

"You're hurt," I said, both worried about her and, embarrassingly, a little grossed out to grab someone's bloody hand. I know, I know. That's the last thing I should have been thinking about at that moment. But, hey, what do you want from me? I was only twelve and a half at the time.

"And you're going to be hurt worse if those guys get to you. C'mon!"

She wiggled her fingers at me impatiently and I reached up and grabbed her wounded hand. She gave a little groan of pain and then pulled me up through the ceiling. I looked around as Karen jumped up and ran noisily across the roof, each hit of her feet shaking the thin metal. We were on top of a five-story-high building. There was nowhere to go.

"What do we do now?" I yelled over to Karen, who was taking the coil of rope off her shoulder.

"I'm doing it," she yelled back. "Guard the hole!"

"What? *How?*"

She turned and sidearmed the metal pole across the roof at me. It clattered up to my feet and before I had a chance to wonder what she was talking about, an octopus guard's head popped up through the hole. I screamed in an embarrassing manner, then quickly picked up the pole and hit the octopus right on top of its fly-eye. The octopus gave its high-pitched whistle of pain and dropped back down into the hole. But just as quickly two tentacle arms reached

through the hole and suctioned onto the roof. I hit them hard with the pole and they let go and disappeared back inside. But immediately another head popped up through the hole. I kept hitting the heads and they kept falling down and popping back up, like the world's easiest but most disturbing game of Whack-a-Mole.

I looked back at Karen and saw that she had tied the rope into a kind of lasso and was getting ready to throw it at the skyscraper across from the theater, aiming it at a flagpole that was flying a flag with Mr. Arthur's face on it.

As Karen flung the lasso onto the flagpole, a tentacle popped up through the hole and grabbed the metal pole out of my hand. An octopus head came up and said, "Let's see how *you* like it!" It then swung the metal pole at me.

Fortunately, all the times as a little kid I had been made fun of for jumping rope with the girls paid off because I immediately leaped in the air, just avoiding the metal pole that would have easily broken both my legs. I turned and saw Karen pulling the rope tight as the octopus guy shot straight up through the hole and landed in a battle pose, brandishing the metal pole like a weapon.

"Here I come!" I yelled as I sprinted over to Karen. She climbed onto the edge of the roof and tensed her grip on the rope, positioning herself to swing. I dived toward the rope as the octopus ran after me, grabbed it just above Karen's hands, and suddenly we were swinging directly toward the windows of the skyscraper, five stories above the street.

The octopus guard flew through the air after us but didn't jump far enough. As we swung at the window I heard the sound of squeaking glass and saw the octopus sliding down the skyscraper's windows, trying desperately to get his suction cups to stick.

Before I could see if he was successful or not, Karen yelled, "Stick out your legs!"

## 31

## SMASH!!!

The window shattered and we flew through the cloud of exploding glass and landed heavily on our backs inside a big empty office.

"Ow!" was about all I could say as I tried to get back the breath that had just been knocked out of me.

. . . SMACK SMACK SMACK SMACK SMACK SMACK SMACK SMACK SMACK . . .

Karen and I exchanged a look as we heard the mysterious sound outside the broken window. Suddenly, a tentacle popped up and slapped down onto the floor. Apparently the octopus had gotten his grip on the windows after all. As another tentacle slapped down and his fly-head popped up,

Karen and I bolted out of the office, slamming the door behind.

**BLAM!** The office door broke open behind us as we tore around the corner and saw an open elevator.

"Oh, man, I always swore I'd never get into one of those in this frequency," Karen said as we sprinted toward the junky-looking elevator and jumped inside. The elevator bounced up and down as we landed, like it was being held up by a bungee cord instead of a steel cable. We looked and saw the octopus come flying around the corner, slipping on the floor and smashing into the wall. His tentacles scrambled on the carpeting and soon he was tearing straight toward us.

"Push the button!" Karen yelled as she reached past me and hit the "1" button over and over. The doors didn't close, even when I started frantically pushing the "close door" button. Oh, man, this might not have been a very good idea, I thought as I stood in the tiny room-on-cables with a murderous octopus running toward us at a very high rate of speed. Just as the octopus guard leaped into the air and flew toward us with his tentacles reaching out and his suction cups smacking at us like four sets of kissing lips, the door went *ding!* and slid closed.

**WHAM!** We heard the octopus hit the door hard as the elevator started to move. I was about to say "That was close!" to Karen when we both realized that the elevator was not going down.

"What the . . . ?" Karen said as she looked at the buttons and started hitting the "1" again. Nope. This elevator was going up. Way up.

7, 8, 9, 10 . . . The numbers lit up on the counter as we watched helplessly. I hit the "stop" button but it didn't respond. . . . 20, 21, 22, 23 . . .

"At least he thinks we're going down," I said, trying to put some kind of positive spin on all this.

"The numbers on his counter are probably showing that we're going up," said Karen, sounding worried for the first time since I'd known her. "God, is everything Arthur built a total piece of junk?"

. . . 50, 51, 52, 53 . . . We were almost at the top, since the buttons only went up to 60. *Only!* Sixty stories above the ground in a building that I knew was a swaying piece of bad engineering with a ton of army guys surrounding it.

Suddenly Frank Gutenkunitz didn't sound so bad.

*DING!* The elevator ground loudly to a stop and bounced up and down so violently that Karen and I fell against each other. The door slid halfway open and then got stuck. Karen pressed the "1" button again, hoping that maybe the elevator would go back down. It made a loud buzzing noise that didn't sound like it was telling us anything good was about to happen.

Karen and I looked at each other and both silently decided that it seemed like a good idea to get out of this dangerous little room. We stepped out cautiously and looked around, in case any of the army guys had somehow beaten us to the top. It was quiet, with only a few flickering lights showing us the crooked hallway. Not sure what to do, we started down the hall, trying to find a stairway.

"So why didn't Arthur want you killed?" she asked as we walked. "What, are you, like, his best friend now or something?"

"Yeah, we're best buddies," I said sarcastically. "He just likes me because I didn't say anything mean to him."

"Why didn't you? You saw what he did to Herfta's city."

"Yeah, like I'm going to give him a hard time when I'm trapped in his house. I didn't want to get thrown into his dungeon."

"So you just kissed his butt? 'Ooo, Mr. Arthur, you're so cool! It's really great how you're forcing a whole frequency of creatures to do everything you say or you'll throw them in jail!' That's pretty pathetic, Iggy."

My face got all hot as I suddenly felt really angry. "Look, I'm not some wannabe kung fu warrior like you, okay? I don't know how to fight and I'm not good at being mean to people. What, did you want me to kick him in the nuts, too, and then take on his whole army?"

"That's what I did."

"Okay, so you're cooler than I am! God! I'm just trying to stay alive right now."

"Sometimes you gotta call people on it when they're doing messed-up stuff, Iggy," she said with a shrug. "You like Foo and you saw her entire city destroyed and yet you meet the guy who was responsible and you don't say anything to him about it."

"I don't think he was responsible," I said, suddenly remembering the conversation I overheard in the gold room.

"What are you talking about?"

"I overheard Mr. Arthur talking to that Herbert Golonski guy and he was yelling at Mr. Arthur for destroying the tree-top city and Mr. Arthur said it wasn't his fault. It sounded like the army did it on their own."

"And you believed him?" she said with a snort.

"Yeah, because Mr. Arthur seemed really upset, and he and that Herbert guy were unloading tons of gold and Herbert was mad because having all the flying people in the air was going to make it hard for him to transport the gold back to our frequency."

Karen stopped and looked at me.

"Wait a minute," she said, looking confused. "*Our* frequency? What gold? And who's that Herbert Golonski guy?"

"Didn't you ever see him when you were hanging with Mr. Arthur?"

"I've never seen him before in my life," she said, looking even more confused. "They're *transporting* gold back to our frequency? How?"

"I don't know. They had piles of gold bars in this big room and they were putting them into some kind of machine that I think can get us back home."

Karen looked really surprised and was about to open her mouth to ask me more questions when suddenly the windows at the end of the hallway exploded inward and three octopus guards flew through and started running toward us.

We both screamed and took off down the hallway. We ran past the elevator, which was still buzzing loudly as the door kept banging, trying unsuccessfully to close itself.

**SMASH!** The window at the other end of the hallway disintegrated into a million pieces as three more octopus guys flew through. We skidded to a stop, trapped. I looked over and saw a door marked STAIRS.

"C'mon!" I said as I grabbed Karen's arm and pulled her away.

I threw open the door and we started running down the winding metal stairs as fast as we could, our footsteps klinking loudly and echoing through the stairwell.

The sound of heavy gorilla feet running fast on the stairs came echoing up to us. Karen and I looked at each other, then she pulled open a door marked 58TH FLOOR and we ran into another hallway.

"They just got out of the stairwell!" we heard a gorilla voice yell as the door closed behind us.

"They're going to find us," Karen said as she looked around for an idea. "We've gotta get out of this building."

"You think the elevator's working yet?" I asked, knowing the answer was no but not having any other ideas.

Karen looked at me and I could see in her eyes that a plan had formed. "Great idea!" she said sincerely. "Let's take the elevator."

I knew from her tone that her new idea of taking the elevator wasn't going to be the standard get-in / press-the-down-button / then-get-off-in-the-lobby version of elevator-taking. She ran around the corner and I heard her kick open an office door. I looked and saw her grabbing tape and mouse pads off a desk. Then she ran out carrying a couple of couch cushions and dropped everything in front of the elevator.

"C'mon!" she said. "Help me open these doors."

I ran over to the elevator and she and I wedged our fingertips into the space where the doors closed and pulled in opposite directions. The doors slid open and a blast of air came out. We peered over the edge. The sixty-story shaft looked like a bottomless pit with a thick rope running down the middle of it.

Before I knew what was happening, Karen grabbed me and started taping one of the couch cushions around my waist, pulling a roll of packing tape around me several times.

"You'll need this padding if you don't want your stomach to get rope-burned," she said as she tore the tape and then started taping the other cushion around her own waist.

"Wait, why would I get rope burns?"

"Because you're going to be sliding down that elevator rope at a very high speed," she said as the sound of the gorilla guards' footsteps got louder inside the stairwell.

"We can't slide down that rope!" I said, really freaking out.

"Maybe you want to take the chance that those guards won't kill you but I don't. So suit yourself," she said as she peered down the shaft again and then looked at the rope to judge how far it was from the edge.

"Wait! You can't just leave me here!" I said, freaking out even more, if such a thing was possible.

"Then follow me."

"But . . . what about our hands?" I asked, desperate to find a way to talk her out of this particular escape plan of hers.

She smiled and held up the mouse pads she had taken from the office. "Arthur's such an idiot. He invented mouse pads before he invented the mouse."

She quickly taped one pad around each of her palms as we heard a gorilla in the stairwell say, "You guys check the fifty-eighth floor. We'll go up to the fifty-ninth."

"Oh, man," I whined. "If I die, I'm gonna kill you."

I held out my hands to Karen and she quickly taped a mouse pad around each of my palms.

The stairway door down the hall burst open. Karen gave me a look that said "Well, here's goes nothin'" and then jumped into the elevator shaft, grabbing onto the rope and sliding down it quickly.

Just then, the gorillas ran around the corner and stopped when they saw me. They smiled and raised their swords threateningly as the octopus guys appeared behind them.

"End of the line, Anti-Art," said the head gorilla guard.

"Wait, Mr. Arthur said not to kill me."

The gorilla looked around at the others, then back at me.

"Don't remember hearing that," he said with a slow shake of his head.

They all started to stalk forward with evil smiles on their faces. I looked at the open shaft, then at the rope. Oh, well, I lied to myself, maybe it'll be fun.

And with that, I jumped into the shaft and grabbed onto the rope. ***Ka-CHUNK!*** The rope jolted and I looked up to see that my weight had dislodged the elevator. It started to move downward as I quickly slid down the rope. I looked up to see the gorillas and octopus guys peering over the edge at me, then almost get their heads cut off by the descending elevator.

I was sliding down the rope quickly and could feel the heat from the friction through the mouse pads. It was getting hot fast. Wisps of smoke started to come out from under them.

"My hands are burning!" I yelled to Karen, who was sliding down the rope about ten stories below me.

"Then stop for a second," she yelled back.

I tightened my grip on the rope and stopped suddenly, which made my hands burn even more. Fortunately the rope was attached to the bottom of the descending elevator so that even when I stopped I was still going down. Just not fast enough. I waved one hand at a time in the air to cool it off, then started to slide down again. What would happen when we got to the bottom? I suddenly wondered. The elevator was coming down fast and unless we got to the bottom with enough time to pull the doors open and get out, we were going to get crushed.

As much as the sliding made my hands burn, the thought of getting smashed flat as a pancake at the bottom of a dirty elevator shaft burned even worse. I loosened my grip on the rope and slid even faster. I heard Karen's feet hit the bottom of the shaft and realized I was almost there.

"Iggy! C'mon! I can't open the door without you!"

*THUMP!* I hit the ground at the bottom of the shaft really hard and my hands felt like they were on fire. I jumped up and started pulling on the doors with Karen. They were shut tight and we were having no luck at all. It probably didn't help that our hands were sore and had the remnants of melted mouse pads on them.

I looked up and saw the elevator coming down really fast now. It was only about ten stories above our heads. I've never been good at math but by my calculations at that moment, I figured we had about zero time left to live.

Just then, we felt a spray of dirt hit us and saw a feel's head sticking up through a trap door in the ground.

"Quick! In here!" he yelled at me as he looked up and saw the elevator almost on top of us.

Before we could even think, Karen and I dived in.

*Slam! BOOM!* The trapdoor dropped shut as the elevator landed on top of it like a ten-ton weight. Karen and I both looked up to see that the feel was standing next to one of the extendable one-eyed weasels, who was holding a lighted torch in his hand. They stared at us, then looked at each other and smiled at Karen like she was a movie star.

"Welcome to the Underground, Anti-Art," said the feel.

I had no idea if they were good guys or bad guys, but considering we would have been dead without them, I sure was happy to see them.

# 32

## NUTS FROM THE UNDERGROUND

As we sat around in the small dirt room that was shaped like the inside of someone's stomach, I kept thinking about how we got there; the bizarre network of underground tunnels, all barely big enough for us to crawl through one at a time; the heavy wet air that smelled like the inside of my grandma's closet; my desperate attempt to not completely freak out because of how claustrophobic it all was. It felt like we crawled through those tunnels for hours even though it was probably a lot less than that. I guess time just passes slower when you can't see where you are and have no idea where the heck you're going.

The feel, whose name was Peepup, and the weasel, who called himself Feep Feep, crawled ahead of us the whole time with their torches lighting the way. But since I was at the back of the pack, all I really saw ahead of me were the silhouettes of Karen, Peepup, and Feep Feep's butts and absolutely nothing behind me. I kept wondering if the guards were going to come through the tunnel after us but figured that when the elevator hit the bottom as hard as it did, the guards must have decided that we were just two really flat, bloody pancakes underneath the elevator's floor that would be too gross to look at. And even if they did decide to look and found we were gone and saw the door to the tunnel, they were all way too big to fit inside it.

Peepup (if you want to say his name in feel language, just stick your lips way out like you're going to kiss someone and then start making popping sounds) told us that the mole creatures had built all the tunnels over the course of many centuries. When I asked him how the mole people could possibly fit inside these because their bodies were so much bigger than the tunnels, he told me that the mole people's bodies were made up of these weird bones and muscles that allowed them to get really long and skinny when they were underground. He said that one of the reasons the members of the Underground traveled around in the mole tunnels was that none of the creatures in Mr. Arthur's army could fit inside them, not even the mole guys.

It seemed that once mole guys joined the army, Mr. Arthur made them all exercise and work out and become bigger and stronger and in doing so, the mole guys' muscles became so hard that they could no longer collapse them enough to get inside their own tunnels. So Peepup and Feep Feep and the others were pretty safe from Mr. Arthur's army when they were in the tunnels, although it meant that the Underground could only really be made up of feels, weasels, and mole creatures who didn't work out.

Okay, I got ahead of myself there. You don't even know what the Underground is. Well . . .

"We are a group of freethinking, nonconformist rebels who have forsaken the tyranny of President Chester Arthur and his authoritarian ways," said Peepup as he handed Karen and me each cups of some hot liquid that looked a lot like mud.

"That's right," said Feep Feep the weasel as he held out a plate covered with roundish cookies that sort of looked like a balls of clay. "We are the leaders of the Underground, who have dedicated our lives to the overthrow of the Arthurian government and the return of the unrestricted society of the pre-Chesterian days."

"Right on!" said Karen excitedly, using a phrase I had only heard used by my uncle, who was a hippie in the 1960s. "How many people are in the Underground?"

Peepup and Feep Feep looked at each other for a second, then sort of lost all the bravado they had had just moments earlier.

"Um . . . just us," said Feep Feep, looking a little embarrassed.

"Well," said Peepup, giving Feep Feep a dirty look, "we're the only ones left at the moment. But there used to be a lot of us."

"What happened?" asked Karen as I tried to drink a mouthful of the hot mud and very secretly spit it back into the cup because it tasted like . . . well . . . a cup of hot mud.

"What do you *think* happened?" asked Peepup. "They were all arrested."

"How did they find out about you?" Karen asked as she took a bite of the clay cookie and didn't seem at all affected by its terrible, Play-Doh-like taste. "Did you guys stage a protest or something?"

"We didn't do anything," said Feep Feep. "We had a few meetings and tried to recruit others to the cause but one by one our members started disappearing. We lost all our diggers or, as you call them, mole guys, first. Mr. Arthur's army saw a few of them leaving our meeting one day and arrested them. Then the rest of them started disappearing one by one, presumably because they were also members of the Underground. But the weird thing was a lot of other diggers who had nothing to do with us and who were actually quite happy living under Mr. Arthur's regime started getting taken away by the army, too, usually for some reason that didn't make any sense. They arrested hundreds of them. We heard that a lot of them were getting nabbed because the army said they simply looked like they were *thinking* bad things about Mr. Arthur."

"Were they only arresting diggers?" Karen asked as she sat forward, looking surprised.

Peepup told us that at first it was just the diggers who were being taken away, but then suddenly the giant babies, whom they called the waddlers, also started getting arrested in large numbers and disappearing. Other creatures also got arrested, but it seemed like Mr. Arthur's army was mostly concerned with the moles and the giant babies.

"You know anything about Herbert Golonski?" Karen asked.

"Who's Herbert Golonski?" asked Peepup with a perplexed look.

"This weird guy who works with Mr. Arthur. He's kind of short and wears a suit. You've never seen him?" I asked.

"Never," said Feep Feep. "Who is he?"

"We don't know," Karen said with a shrug. "I never saw him before, either. But he's not a good guy."

"Where does the army put all the diggers and waddlers after they're arrested?" I asked.

"We have no idea," said Feep Feep. "A couple of times we sent one of our scouts to follow the army when they took some of the diggers away but then we'd never hear from the scouts again, either. We just assumed they got arrested and put in prison, too. Wherever prison is."

"Did you see any of them when you were locked up in the White House?" I asked Karen.

"No," she said, perplexed. "I was in a small cell in the basement but there weren't enough cells to hold more than a few people."

"Then maybe this has something to do with the gold mines," I said, trying to figure it all out.

"What gold mines?" said Peepup and Feep Feep in unison as they gave me a perplexed look.

*    *    *

Man, did my knees hurt.

That was all I could think about as we crawled through an endless maze of tunnels for what I think actually *was* hours this time. When I told them about the gold in the secret room and the weird machine and what I had heard Herbert Golonski telling Mr. Arthur about transporting the gold from the mines to the White House, they all wanted to find out just where these mines were and what this gold business was all about. Karen was getting really riled up at the thought that on top of everything else Mr. Arthur had done to this frequency, he could now add stealing gold to the list. Peepup and Feep Feep didn't really understand it all, since gold wasn't really something that any of the creatures in this frequency knew or cared about. They had seen it from time to time because the mole people would occasionally come across chunks of gold when they were digging their tunnels, but except for occasionally using a piece as decoration somewhere, it was about as important to them as dandelions were to us back home.

But everybody decided we should try to find the mines, so that maybe we could figure out exactly what was going on in Lesterville, who exactly this Herbert Golonski guy was, and where all their friends were. And so I changed out of my pajamas back into my regular clothes and we were suddenly crawling through the endless maze of mole tunnels that led everywhere in the city. Which was why my knees were hurting so badly.

As we crawled along, Peepup and Feep Feep told us that in the centuries before Mr. Arthur arrived, the mole people, the giant babies, the praying mantises, the feels, the weasels, and all the other creatures I had originally seen at the Artbucks lived in the valley where Lesterville is now, and that they all got along pretty well. They each had their own languages and different ways of living but they tried to learn bits of the others' languages so that they could have a basic understanding of one another. A few generations back they all pitched in and built a village in order to protect themselves against the gorilla guys and the octopus guys and the potato bug guys, all of whom lived in the next valley over and were pretty aggressive. They would occasionally come into this valley and steal food because the dirt in their valley wasn't as good at growing plants as it was over here.

When the creatures in this valley weren't all together in a village, they had a hard time fighting off the gorillas and octopuses and potato bugs. But once they were all bonded together, they were able to scare the bad guys away because they outnumbered them and, to put it frankly, the bad guys were sort of stupid. And so the bad guys pretty much stayed in their not-so-great valley and things over here were pretty nice.

Then Mr. Arthur showed up and at first everybody loved him. They were really into the idea of learning a language they could all use to communicate with each other, since they could never decide on one language between themselves and it was hard for them to learn all the different languages they each spoke. So they really took to Mr. Arthur teaching them English (even though he decided to call it

Artlish) and some of them even got quite fluent in it, like Peepup and Feep Feep. And then when Mr. Arthur started showing the creatures all the other ideas he had (that he said were all things he was thinking up on the spot), they really felt like he was the super smart leader they never had. The creatures did everything he said and helped him start to construct new buildings and stores and acted in his plays and listened to his music. And so things were pretty good.

But then everything started to change.

Mr. Arthur started to get really weird if he heard anybody talking in any language other than Artlish because he never took the time to learn any of their languages and didn't like not being able to understand what they were saying. And he started to get mad if they didn't want to do something he told them to do. And he got really mad if anybody didn't like one of his plays or songs or if they wouldn't wear the clothes he was making. And while they didn't like getting him mad, if there was something he wanted them to do that they didn't want to do, then they simply wouldn't do it.

And that was about the time the army showed up.

One day, a bunch of the gorilla guys and octopus guys and potato bug guys marched and rolled into town, wearing uniforms and telling everybody that they'd better do everything Mr. Arthur said or they'd be in trouble. Nobody could believe it. And they didn't know what to do because now the bad guys all had swords and axes and spinning blades and other dangerous weapons that they were willing to use on anybody who didn't do what they told them. A few of the creatures tried to stand up to them but they were quickly "made examples of."

Suddenly the fun-filled town of Lesterville became a pretty scary place. Since no one was used to living under such unpleasant conditions, many of them simply decided that life would be easier if they just did what Mr. Arthur and the army told them to do. And so Mr. Arthur started making them build more and more buildings and watch more and more plays and wear more and more clothes and "enjoy" anything else he invented or told them to do.

This was the world into which Karen and I both arrived.

When I asked them about the flying people and if they hated them like Herbert Golonski had said they did, Peepup said that while none of the creatures in this valley really cared one way or the other about the flying people (they didn't dislike them but they didn't really like them, either, since the flying people would never interact with them or even wave hello when they flew over the city), the guys in the army from the other valley really hated them. Apparently the flying people would fly into the gorilla guys' valley all the time and take the water from their lake without ever saying a word or asking if it was okay. There was more than enough water for the gorillas and octopuses and potato bugs, but they still got really mad that the flying people were taking it all the time without their permission.

So it started to make sense to me that, given the opportunity to start chopping down some of the flying people's trees yesterday, there was a very good chance that the gorillas and octopuses and potato bugs would simply destroy the whole city, just because they had waited generations to get back at the flying people.

When I asked why there were some creatures from this valley in the army, like the mole commander, Feep Feep said that there were always some members of the village who weren't the nicest creatures in the world. And since it's impossible that any group of people would be all good and all nice, the minute those creatures saw the power that the army had and all their weapons and uniforms, they immediately joined up and turned out to be some of the meanest members of Mr. Arthur's force.

It was right about this time we finally got to an opening over our heads in the tunnel that Peepup said came out behind the White House. He made a "be quiet" face to us and carefully pushed up on the boards that were covering the tunnel's entrance. Peepup peeked out of the door and said that there were no guards around that he could see. Then we all nervously stood up and peered out.

It was still dark, even though the sun was just beginning to light up the sky as it slowly made its way toward the horizon. We looked across the field and saw a small path that went up and over a hill that stood between the White House and the mountains in the distance.

"I used to see that path when I was staying in that stupid White House," said Karen as she furrowed her brow. "Never thought anything of it. That must be the route they bring the gold in on."

Just as she said that, we saw a cart that was covered with a dark cloth come over the hill, being pushed with great effort by two giant babies. One of the babies had a big white spot on its forehead that stood out as the first glow of the dawn light hit it.

"Hey, look," said Feep Feep as he squinted to see the big purple baby. "Isn't that Mmph?"

Peepup strained his neck forward, as if the extra couple of inches would help him see better. "Yeah, and that's Hmm next to him."

Then one of the rolling potato bugs came over the hill behind them, spinning the wagon wheel with the blades on it as we heard the faint sound of him saying, "C'mon, keep moving," in this really weird rumbly voice.

"They're slaves?" said Karen, more to herself than to the rest of us.

"Mmph and Hmm wouldn't be working for them because they *wanted* to," said Peepup, shaking his head in disbelief. "They hated the army more than any of our other members."

"Chester's running a *labor* camp?" Karen said to herself again, although she said it so loudly and angrily it could easily have been intended for the rest of us to hear.

Just then, the gold cart hit a rise in the path and got stuck. The babies pushed to get it over the hump but were having trouble. The guard's eye got a mean look and he rolled full force into the waddler nearest him, knocking the big baby hard into the back of the cart. The baby made a low bassy sound of pain, and then pushed with all his might. The cart rolled over the hump and they continued pushing it down the path.

I looked at Karen, Peepup, and Feep Feep. They all looked pretty angry.

We had to do something. This wasn't how things should have been in this frequency.

I just had no idea what we were going to do.

# 33

# WORKIN' IN A GOLD MINE

The sun had now come up over the horizon and its golden rays were beginning to light up the hill as we slowly and carefully crawled through the tall thick reddish grass. We could see that there were guards up on top of the White House who would occasionally look over to make sure nobody was sneaking through the field, which was exactly what we were doing. Unfortunately, there were no tunnels that led this way for us to hide in as we moved and, even if there were, we had no idea where we were going. The area over the hill was a place the creatures of Lesterville never went, since it led toward the valley where the gorilla guys came from. Ever since Mr. Arthur started up his army, nobody from Lesterville ever came anywhere near the White

House and wouldn't dare try to go into the fields and hills behind it. It was just easier and safer to stay in town and not cause trouble.

It took us quite a while to get to the top of the hill, since we had to stay so low to the ground and keep checking back to make sure the guards weren't watching. Fortunately, they didn't really seem to care too much about things on the ground at that moment and were scanning the skies most of the time, which I assumed meant they were keeping an eye out for the flying people. I honestly didn't know why Herbert Golonski cared about the flying people seeing what he was doing with his gold mine, since the flying people didn't care what happened on the ground. But I guess, knowing that their entire city had been destroyed by Mr. Arthur's army, Golonski must have figured that the flying people might be mad enough to take some kind of revenge.

I looked up at the sky. It was empty.

"Where's Foo?" I whispered to Karen. "I thought she was helping us."

"Don't get attached to her," said Karen. "The flying people are weird. They're your friends one day and then the next day they act like they don't even know you. Foo wanted to help me get you out of Arthur's house and then she disappeared. All the flying people disappeared. Just when you'd think they would want to stand up for themselves and get involved, they all just fly away. They care so little about things on the ground that they're willing to just leave even after the army attacked them and destroyed everything they had. I don't think I'll ever understand them."

I thought it was kind of weird, too, until I remembered that we had a bird's nest in our backyard last year that our neighbor's cat climbed up to and knocked off the tree branch. The nest fell onto the ground and then the cat ate the eggs that were in it. It was really gross and sad and I kept wondering if the bird whose nest was destroyed was going to come and attack the cat or rebuild the nest in our tree again. But it never did. My dad ended up accidentally running the nest over with his lawn mower and the bird never rebuilt his or her house in our tree. So I had to figure that maybe things that can fly, whether they're animals or people, just find it easier to cut their losses and move on.

I guess if I could fly, it'd be really easy to just fly away from my problems, which in a way I tried to do when I built that rocket. And it worked, because I definitely left the problems I was worried about, like Frank Gutenkunitz and all the mean kids in my school, back in our frequency. But then I found a whole new world of problems.

Man, sometimes I feel like I can't do anything right.

Before I could think too much about all this, we got to the top of the hill, which was good because instead of thinking about all my little problems I immediately saw that there were a lot of creatures who were having some really *big* problems.

Stretching out before us in the valley was what looked like a huge prison camp. There was a big scary fence running around the place and lots of guards on watch. Inside the fence was this huge area that looked like some sort of coal mine or something. There were mountains of dirt piled everywhere and tons of holes in the ground. We saw lots of mole creatures crawling in and out of the holes. The ones who were coming out pushed big buckets of dirt ahead of them, which giant babies took and dumped out into these big trays that had mesh on the bottom. The babies then picked up the trays and shook them back and forth so that the dirt sifted through the mesh and then there'd be a bunch of pieces of gold left inside.

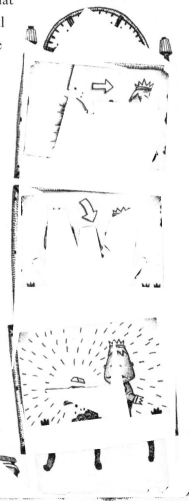

The babies then took the trays and dumped the gold pieces into these big heavy bowls that were sitting over fires. The gold melted as some weasels and feels stirred the pots with big metal poles. They then poured the gold into molds. When the gold cooled off, they turned over the molds and gold bars dropped out. Finally, the babies picked up the gold and put it on this big thing that sort of looked like a huge bathroom scale.

Standing next to the scale was Herbert Golonski! He was holding a pad of paper and looked at the readout on the scale and wrote down something on his pad and then the babies took the gold bars off the scale and piled them up on carts and covered the carts with cloth and then two of them would push the cart out of an opening in the fence that led to the path. They were always followed by one of the guards, who yelled at them and threatened him with his weapon and pushed them and generally did mean stuff, even though it didn't look like the babies really needed anyone to tell them to push the cart since they didn't seem to have much choice in the matter, anyway.

"There's all our friends!" said Feep Feep in a loud whisper.

"This is unbelievable!" was all that Karen could say as she stared at the gold camp with her mouth hanging open. And she was right. It was pretty crazy.

***BA-BOOF!*** Suddenly dirt exploded up from everywhere as a bunch of gorilla guards jumped up out of their own secret tunnels in the ground and landed in a circle around us. Then they pointed their swords at us, the gleaming sharp tips about one inch from our heads.

We were officially in big trouble.

# 34

# THE GOLD HITS THE FAN

"Well, well, well. If it isn't the Anti-Art."

We looked and saw Mr. Arthur coming over the hill. A bunch of gorilla guards were behind him, as well as the big baby who had been guarding the White House gate. The waddler was wearing his suit and tie and had on a big pair of sunglasses so that he looked like a huge, swollen version of a secret service agent.

"Hello, Karen," said Mr. Arthur as he stepped through the guards and stood in front of her. However, he suddenly seemed to remember what had happened the last time he had gotten too close to her and so quickly pulled one of the gorilla guards in front of him for protection. "Long time no see."

"Yeah, long enough to open a gold mine and turn lots of your loyal subjects into slaves," she said to him with a look of contempt on her face.

"Those aren't loyal subjects. They're people who broke the law."

"What'd they do?" she asked with a smirk. "Not kiss your butt enough?"

I saw Peepup and Feep Feep exchange a look between them that showed they couldn't believe Karen was talking to Mr. Arthur that way. And Mr. Arthur clearly wasn't too happy about it, either.

"I'm trying to be nice here," said Mr. Arthur, looking annoyed. "I could have you working down there in two seconds if I wanted to. You've broken the law more than any of them."

"You're unbelievable, Chester," she said as she shook her head. "I really think you've lost your mind. You're stealing *gold* now?"

This seemed to throw him. He got a surprised look, then said, "I'm not stealing anything."

"Yeah? What are you doing, then? Just digging up all that shiny yellow stuff because you think it looks pretty?"

"I needed something for the prisoners to do and it was decided that we might as well mine the gold out of there, since there's so much of it."

"And who decided that? Herbert Golonski? Where did

that guy come from? What, was he in the house with you when you blew it up?"

"No," said Mr. Arthur, starting to sound like he was getting mad.

"Then who is he?"

"None of your business."

"What are you, five?" she said with a snort. "Sorry to make you talk about your boyfriend."

"Hey, he's a boy and he's my friend but he's not my boyfriend!" Mr. Arthur snapped at her, sounding very much like Ivan's little sister at that moment. He then looked around at the guards self-consciously. You could tell this conversation wasn't really going the way he had planned. "And *I* make all the decisions around here. You got that? I'm the *president*, you know."

"Yeah, you're one hell of a president." She laughed. "Gold's not even worth anything here, you know. The creatures couldn't care less about it."

"If I *say* it's worth something, it is. Gold's only valuable in our frequency because a long time ago somebody decided it should be."

"So that's your goal as president?" Karen laughed. "To make gold valuable here?"

"Hey, I'd worry a little more about yourself right now," Mr. Arthur said, losing patience. "Because you are in big trouble."

Karen just shook her head and gave him the you're-an-idiot look. "I thought you were pathetic because you turned this village into some kind of plagiarized vanity project, but now I find out you're just doing it to get rich back in our frequency? That's really lame, man, even for you."

Mr. Arthur stared at her, thrown. "I'm not taking gold back to our frequency."

"That's not what I heard."

Mr. Arthur looked at me, immediately figuring out that I was the one who told her and looking a bit freaked out that I had discovered his secret operation. Then he leaned in to us and whispered in a really exasperated voice, "Look, I didn't even come up with that plan, okay? It was Herbert."

Karen stared at Mr. Arthur for a second, then burst out laughing. "You're such a loser, Chester. Even when you're doing something evil, it's not your own idea."

Mr. Arthur stared at her with his mouth hanging open like someone had just sucked all the air out of his lungs. All the guards kept glancing at each other, then back at Mr. Arthur, wondering what he was going to do next. Or *if* he was going to do anything next.

Which was right when Herbert Golonski walked through the crowd of guards.

"Mr. President, you're not going to let anyone talk to you like that, are you?" Herbert said as he shook his head like a teacher who had just found out you had cheated on an exam. "Especially not a criminal."

"Hey, Chester, your boyfriend's back," Karen said with a smirk. "Maybe he brought you a gold necklace or something."

Herbert looked at Karen, walked up to her, and smiled. But it was one of those smiles that said he didn't think she was funny. "Your president is a very fair and patient man, my dear. But I wouldn't expect his patience to last much longer."

"Okay," Karen said slowly as she narrowed her eyes at Herbert, "first of all, he's not *my* president, nor is he the president of anything. He's just some failure who tried to blow himself up and because of that, he ended up in this frequency where he is now passing off all the best achievements of actual smart and talented people as his own. Second, if I'm the criminal, how come it's you who's stealing gold from this place? And third . . ."

**CRACK!** Karen kneed Herbert extremely hard right in the groin. He made a sound like a sea lion and doubled over in agony. I have to admit, even though he was a jerk, I sort of felt sorry for the guy at that moment.

". . . I'm not your 'dear,'" Karen said, finishing her sentence.

As Herbert rolled around on the ground trying to catch his breath through what had to have been major pain, the guards all tensed up on their weapons, which were now even closer to our faces.

"Oh, man, I should have warned you," Mr. Arthur said as he bent down to help Herbert. "She did that same exact thing to me once."

Mr. Arthur tried to help Herbert stand up but Herbert just pushed him away angrily, his face red with pain. "Aren't you going to do anything, Arthur? Are you going to let her get away with this? What kind of a world are you running here, anyway? Look around! Look at your guards! You know what they see? They see an ineffective leader. They see a pushover. And unless you make an example out of this—" Herbert pointed at Karen like she was a monster. "—*Anti-Art*, then you can kiss any and all security goodbye. Because if no one's afraid of you, then no one's going to do what you tell them to do. Not your people, not your guards, not your army. No one!" Herbert then struggled shakily to his feet, still clearly feeling the pain of Karen's knee. He grabbed Mr. Arthur by the collar, got in his face, and said quietly enough that he thought Karen and I couldn't hear, "And if no one's doing what you tell them to do, then I can't get this gold out of here!"

Mr. Arthur stared at Herbert, looking both afraid and unsure what to do. He was clearly intimidated by this Herbert Golonski guy. Then he suddenly puffed himself up, trying to be tough again.

"You bet I'm going to do something." Mr. Arthur turned to the guards. "Lock her up in the White House prison. Right now."

Two of the gorilla guards grabbed Karen's hands and held them behind her back. She tried to pull out of their grasp but they were just too strong.

**CLICK-CLICK!** Another guard behind Karen snapped a huge set of handcuffs tightly around her wrists. The two guards held her by her upper arms as she struggled to get away.

"Let go of me!" she yelled as she thrashed about. However, she quickly slowed her struggling because I could see the handcuffs were cutting into her wrists as she fought. Seeing Karen with her hands locked behind her back and being subdued by the guards made me suddenly feel really sad, like the time Gary's mom had their cat — who used to scratch us and attack us like crazy — declawed. We thought we'd be happy to be safe from her sharp nails but the first time we saw her try to jump from the couch to hang on the drapes and she slid down and crashed to the floor, we all felt really bad. It was sort of like even though we were scared of her with claws, she had lost her dignity without them. And that's something you never want to see happen to anybody, no matter how mean they can occasionally be.

Well, maybe except for Frank Gutenkunitz. I'll have to get back to you on that one.

Herbert watched all this, then turned to Mr. Arthur again. Herbert had a really mean look on his face that showed he was getting mad at everybody.

"Get *rid* of her, Chester," Herbert hissed in Mr. Arthur's face. "She already escaped once from your ridiculous prison. She's never going to be anything but trouble. This girl has been running around for a year trying to turn people against you. Be a man, Arthur! Be a leader! Take her down to the square, bring everybody out, tell them this is what happens if they disobey you or try to do anything against your leadership . . . and then cut off her head."

Karen's eyes went wide. Even though she had always been cool under pressure, the idea that someone might actually kill her seemed to throw her quite a bit. As it did me. *And* Mr. Arthur.

"K-kill her?" Mr. Arthur said, the words sticking in his throat like saltine crackers when you try to swallow a bunch of them without any water.

"Yes! What do you think you're doing? Playing games? Leaders have to take charge and they have to do ruthless things in order to stay in power. Haven't you ever read Machiavelli? You can't make people follow you unless they're afraid of you. And they can't be afraid of you unless they really think you will do something terrible to them if they don't do what you want them to do! So do it, Arthur! Execute her!"

Mr. Arthur stared at Herbert with a very serious look on his face. Then he looked at Karen, and then at me. I couldn't tell what he was thinking but his face looked like he was really considering what Herbert had just said. It was a scary look, sort of like when Mr. Haleran, our English teacher who was a really nice guy and who never got mad at anybody, found out that lots of kids had stopped doing their homework because they said he was too much of a wimp to yell at them or give them a bad grade. He came into class after hearing that and was a completely different person, really intense and angry, like whatever had been nice inside him sort of died upon hearing the news that everybody was taking advantage of him. Unfortunately, Mr. Arthur looked like he was thinking it might be time to prove something to the world.

I knew that if Mr. Arthur decided to take Herbert's advice and tell the guards to execute Karen, he wouldn't be able to turn back, even if he wanted to. He was too worried about being president and keeping his little world going and he was too much under the spell of Herbert to say no to him once he had already said yes. And I knew that I didn't have the skills or powers to do what people always did in these situations in the movies, where someone they know is standing on the gallows and is about to be hung and all of a sudden they come riding in on a horse and shoot the rope with a gun so that their friend just falls to the ground and is safe and then some army rides in and saves the day. I didn't have an army and I didn't have a gun and I couldn't shoot it if I did. I didn't have anything to save the day with. All I could think to do was to speak up.

"Mr. Arthur," I said as he looked at me, almost startled to hear my voice, "you can't do this. This isn't why you became president, is it? To have slaves and an army and to make everybody afraid of you? That wasn't who you were back in our school. I know. My friends' brothers and sisters used to know you and they said you were a nice guy. And I always used to look at your picture and feel like I knew you, too. Like I had something in common with you. I know you never felt comfortable in our frequency. Neither did I.

"I don't know if any of your students were ever mean to you, or if you had bullies when *you* were a student, but I know I sure did. I couldn't stand them, how mean they could be to me just because they decided they didn't like me or because I was too nice or too scared to fight back. I never knew why they acted that way but maybe they were trying to prove to me that they were in charge. But I didn't want them to be in charge and the school didn't need them to be in charge. And if they weren't there, our school would have been a nicer place."

Herbert rolled his eyes and sighed. "Arthur, will you shut this kid up and do it already?"

Before anybody could stop me, I kept talking, trying to

make Mr. Arthur realize just how crazy everything had gotten.

"The people in this frequency," I said as Mr. Arthur stared at me, "they all liked you when you first got here. They liked that you taught them a new language and that you were bringing them so many new things. I mean, sure, you probably should have told them that the stuff you were bringing wasn't all stuff you had thought up yourself, but that might even have been okay if you had just given them a choice about whether they wanted to like it or not. But now . . . you've turned into a bully.

"You didn't need to bring in the creatures from the other valley to keep the people of Lesterville in line. Nobody wanted to hurt you. You just needed to protect them from the bad guys. But now you're becoming a bad guy. And the more you do to scare people, the more they're going to hate you. They might act like they like you and they might be afraid to do anything against you for a while, but they're not going to stay that way forever. And then you'll just have to start killing more and more of them.

"Karen only wanted to stop you because she saw how unhappy people were becoming under you. She wanted to save them from their bully. But I just know that deep down, you don't want to be a bully. You've never wanted to be a bully. You just wanted people to like you and like what you do. And they still can. Just, please, don't kill Karen."

I got so wrapped up in what I was saying that I have an embarrassing feeling that I was sort of getting all choked up by the time I got to the end of my speech. I looked over at Karen, who gave me a small, surprised smile, like she was actually impressed with something I had done for the first time ever.

Mr. Arthur stared at me, thinking, as an angry Herbert stepped up in front of him.

"Are we finished playing around now?" he said. "Finished with our little speeches? Because if you don't do this, Chester, then I will."

"But . . . I'm the president," Mr. Arthur said weakly. "I'm in charge here."

"You're not in charge of anything," Herbert said with a laugh. "You've just been the person who's done everything I've told him to do. You're my mouthpiece, and you're a ridiculous one at that. So if you can't even do the simple things I tell you to do, then why don't you go back to your little workshop and play with all your toys and leave the running of important things to the adults."

Mr. Arthur stared at Herbert, then looked at Karen and me.

Then, after a second . . .

### CRACK!

Mr. Arthur kneed Herbert Golonski in the crotch harder than Karen had. Herbert made an even louder sea lion sound and fell over in pain.

"*I* am in charge here," Mr. Arthur said angrily. "This is *my* city and *I* built it and *I* decide what happens here, not you. Got it?" He then turned to the guards as Herbert Golonski lay whimpering on the ground. "Let the girl go."

I looked over at Karen, who seemed very surprised. Then she looked at Mr. Arthur with an impressed expression on her face. As I watched the guard behind Karen take the handcuffs off of Karen's wrists, I noticed something out of the corner of my eye. I looked up at the sky and saw a very strange thing.

A big flaming cloud.

I started to wonder if maybe flaming clouds were just one more of the bizarre things in this frequency when I heard someone running and yelling behind us. We all turned to see a gorilla guard chugging up the hill toward us from the direction of downtown Lesterville.

"They're coming!" he yelled in a panic as he galloped quickly on his three legs. "They say they're going to burn down the city!"

"Who's going to burn down the city?" called Mr. Arthur, looking thrown.

"The flappers!"

The guard pointed at the cloud, which upon closer look was indeed thousands of flying people all heading in a huge formation toward Lesterville, each one of them carrying a lit torch. We could hear the faint sound of someone in the flaming cloud yelling something down at the city but it was too distant to understand.

"Oh, my God . . ." said Mr. Arthur as his mouth dropped open and his eyes went wide. "Get the entire army to the city! NOW!"

And with that, all the guards took off running as fast as they could toward Lesterville as Mr. Arthur bolted past us like his pants were on fire.

The gorilla guards were making loud weird howling noises like sirens as they ran down the hill toward the city. Other army guys started running and rolling from the White House and swarming over hills and streaming out of hiding places. Karen looked down at Herbert, who was still too immobilized by the pain of his crushed testicles to be able to do anything. She turned to Peepup and Feep Feep.

"Keep an eye on him, you guys," she said, pointing at Herbert. "Tie him up if you have to." Then she looked at me and said, "Let's go."

She sprinted off after Mr. Arthur as I looked down at Herbert, who stared up at me with bloodshot eyes and an angry look on his face.

"You have no idea what you are messing with, kid," he said in a scary tone. "No idea."

Now feeling more weirded out by him than I had been before, I turned and ran off after Karen toward the strange city with the huge flaming cloud hovering over it.

# 35

# THE FALL OF THE ARTHURIAN EMPIRE

"ATTENTION, CITIZENS OF LESTERVILLE. PLEASE EVACUATE IMMEDIATELY ANY AND ALL ARTHURIAN BUILDINGS. YOU WILL BE SAFE IN YOUR ORIGINAL DWELLINGS WHICH ARE MADE OUT OF NONFLAMMABLE MATERIALS. I REPEAT, PLEASE EVACUATE ALL NONORIGINAL, ARTHURIAN-MADE BUILDINGS IMMEDIATELY. WE CANNOT BE RESPONSIBLE FOR YOUR SAFETY IF YOU DO NOT EVACUATE."

As we ran into Art's Square, we saw Mr. Arthur's army pouring into the city from all directions.

The creatures of Lesterville were running and slithering and hopping out of the buildings and taking off past the army guys to get away from the square. An eerie orange and red glow lit up the city as the massive blanket of flaming torches hovered above us, making the sky look like it was on fire. I saw Herfta in the center of the flying people, holding some sort of funnel that he was using as a megaphone.

"CHESTER ARTHUR, YOU HAVE ATTACKED OUR PEACEFUL CITY AND DESTROYED IT WITHOUT PROVOCATION. AND SO, AS IS WRITTEN IN PUHLUVIAN LAW, THE SAME TREATMENT SHALL BE ACCORDED TO YOU AND YOUR CITY. PLEASE EVACUATE YOUR CITIZENS IMMEDIATELY."

"No, wait!" yelled Mr. Arthur, who pushed through his army and ran into the center of the square. "What happened to your city was a *mistake!* It was never my intention to destroy anything. We were merely trying to locate two people who we thought were criminals, and things . . . well . . . they got a bit out of hand. We never meant you or your people any ill will."

Herfta hung in the air, burning torch in his hand, his wings slowly flapping. After a few seconds of staring down at Mr. Arthur, he slowly started to descend and said, "It was still your army, wasn't it? And isn't it up to you to control them? Are you saying that you, as president, have no control over your army?"

"No!" Mr. Arthur said a bit too quickly, then immediately tried to regain his composure. "I mean, of course not. I have complete control over them. They follow my orders. I *am* their leader, you know."

"Then it's your fault that they destroyed our city."

"No!" Mr. Arthur said even quicker this time. I noticed that beads of sweat were starting to form on his brow. "I mean, they *didn't* follow my orders. Because I told them to find Karen and Iggy, but I *didn't* tell them to destroy your city."

"So then you *don't* control your army," said Herfta.

"Yes, I do! I mean . . . it's just . . ." Mr. Arthur's voice started to sound more and more unsure. "You know, I just sort of didn't control them at that moment."

"And which moment would that be?" Herfta said sarcastically as he landed in front of Mr. Arthur. "The moment in which our entire city and everything we owned was completely destroyed by your army?"

Mr. Arthur stood there staring at Herfta for a long time. Then, finally, he said, "Uh . . . yeah. That's the moment."

Herfta looked up at all the flying people, who nodded back at him. "Okay, let's burn the place down," he said as he flew quickly back up to them. Then the flying people all raised their torches with a *whoosh* and prepared to throw them down at the buildings.

"Wait!" cried Mr. Arthur as he fell to his knees. "You can't burn it down! It's all I have. It's all I've ever wanted. I realize that I might have gone too far in trying to protect it. I know that I never should have forced things on people and had an army threaten them into liking it all. But I did it for their own good. You can't send them back to the primitive world I first found them in. This . . ." He held out his arms, motioning to all of Lesterville as his eyes started to tear up. "This is good. And the people like it. I know they do. I can see it in their faces whenever I bring them something new. Don't ruin their world just because a mistake of mine caused the destruction of your city. None of us is thinking clearly right now. We can help you rebuild. We can disband the army. Just, *please*, don't destroy my city!"

Mr. Arthur dropped his head and started sobbing. It was pretty embarrassing for everybody, I have to say, especially all the creatures who had spent the last few years being terrified of him. His army exchanged looks that said they were surprised to see their leader crying like this and that it was affecting their impression of him. I mean, there's nothing wrong with crying and all, but this sort of went into the category of desperate whimpering and begging.

"Father! Wait!"

We all looked and saw Foo come flying through the torches and straight down toward us. She spread her wings and came to a halt about ten feet above me, just out of the army creatures' reach.

"FOO!" Herfta yelled. "Get back up here! Right this minute!"

Foo suddenly looked nervous and glanced up at her father. He glared down at her with the expression all dads make when they don't want you to do something they think is stupid. Then she looked at me. I gave her a smile and said, "If you want to say something, Foo, then you should say it."

She stared at me, thinking. Then she smiled, looked up at Herfta, and said, "No, father, I'm going to speak."

Herfta looked stunned, then gave her a rather begrudging nod that said "I'm not happy about this but go ahead."

"Mr. Arthur is right," she said, loud enough so that all the flying people could also hear her. "None of us is thinking clearly right now. You have always taught me that we should never make any decisions out of anger and passion. That we are a rational and fair people, and that this is what makes us the people of the sky. For us to throw that all away on one act of revenge would lessen who we are. And none of us would ever want that to happen."

Foo locked eyes with her father to let him know just how serious she was. Herfta stared at his daughter. It was hard to tell what he was thinking. Mr. Arthur glanced up and sniffled as he looked at Herfta with a "*please* listen to your daughter" look on his face.

"You speak the truth, my girl," Herfta said after a few seconds. He then flew down to Foo, put his hand up, and brushed it against her cheek as Foo smiled at him, proud and relieved. "But the offenses that have been committed against us are grave, more grave than any our people have ever encountered. What would you propose we do?"

Foo turned and looked down at me. "We should let the newcomer decide."

A murmur went up through the flying people, as well as the creatures in the army. Herfta got a surprised look and Karen's mouth dropped open, although I'm sure nobody's face was showing more surprise than mine at that moment.

"Foo, now *you're* letting your emotions get the best of you," Herfta said as he gave me a dirty look. "Just because you like this boy doesn't mean the fate of this city should be decided by him."

Foo made an angry face that made her suddenly look very much like her dad. "Don't insult me, Father," she said sharply. "Whether or not I like the newcomer is irrelevant. The reason I think he should be the one to decide is that he is the only one among us who can truly be fair."

"Wait a minute," said Karen as she stepped forward. "What about me? I've been trying to stop Chester ever since I got here a year ago."

"Which is exactly why you're not the right person to make this decision," Foo said to Karen with a friendly but firm smile. "Iggy is the most open-minded person we have. And . . ." Foo looked down and gave me the same smile she did before she put her hand on my face when we got in trouble with Herfta. "I know that he is a very wise and honest person. He would never do something that wasn't rational."

There's nothing like the feeling you get when thousands of people turn and look at you at the exact same time. Which is exactly what happened at that moment. The flying people, the army, Mr. Arthur, Karen, and all the creatures who lived in Lesterville looked at me from wherever they were standing or flying at that moment. The Lestervillians were all packed into the streets that led out of the square, ready to make a quick escape in case their city was set ablaze.

Karen gave me a look that said "Tell them to burn it down." Mr. Arthur gave me a look that said "Please, tell them *not* to burn it down." The army guys were all giving me looks that said "Why do you suddenly have more power than our president?" And the creatures of Lesterville? Well, I honestly couldn't tell what they were thinking. They seemed to be staring at me with a look that said "If you're the one who's going to decide our fate, then maybe you're going to be our new president and so we don't want to do anything to get on your bad side." I have to say it was a look that made me feel really bad for them, since it was the look of a bunch of people who hadn't gotten to make a decision on their own for a really long time.

Which suddenly made me realize exactly what the answer was to this whole situation.

"Um . . ." I said as I stepped forward. I've never been good at public speaking, anyway, and so doing it right now in front of so many people at such a high-pressure moment was more than terrifying. But I knew that this was one of those times in life when you had to put all your fears and insecurities away and do the right thing. "The only people who can really make this decision and who *should* make this decision are the people who it affects the most. The citizens of Lesterville."

Foo smiled at me as if she approved of my answer. The army all exchanged looks, then stared over at the mass of creatures who were packed into the side streets. Mr. Arthur looked up hopefully. The flying people looked at Herfta, who was considering what I had just said. After a few moments, he looked around at the other flying people, then down at the creatures in the streets.

"Very well. Even though we were given no choice in the matter of the destruction of our city, and even though we, like yourselves, had done nothing to justify the loss of our homes, we, as a fair and rational people, leave it to you, the citizens of Lesterville, to tell us what to do."

There was silence, except for the sound of the army creatures, who were shifting around uncomfortably, clearly unsure of what was about to happen and not at all happy to be standing under the rumbling crackle of thousands of lit torches. The creatures of Lesterville all looked around at each other and considered their decision without speaking. Whatever they were communicating with their eyes seemed to be more important than any words or language at that moment.

Finally, the creatures all looked back at me. Then, softly, I heard them begin to chant.

". . . burn it . . . burn it . . . burn it . . . burn it . . ."

Mr. Arthur's face dropped as the army started to look around at one another and then up at the flying people.

Karen leaned over to Mr. Arthur, clearly unsure how to feel about the realization that her dream of bringing down Mr. Arthur's empire was about to come true in a major way. "Chester, I'd get all your fire equipment ready if I were you."

"We don't have any fire equipment," Mr. Arthur said as he stared blankly, sounding like he was about to start crying. "We don't have anything to fight fires with because I never thought anything bad would ever happen here. And it doesn't really matter anyway . . . because my army is terrified of fire."

As their chant got louder and louder, the Lesterville creatures began to back away down the side streets, moving to safety.

"Burn it, burn it, burn it!" they continued in unison.

The flying people raised their torches, which *whoosh*ed and crackled, and started to come down lower. The army started to back away, looking like nervous cattle in a cowboy movie, as a feel stepped forward out of the Lesterville crowd. He raised his floaty arm and pointed his sucker at the army.

"And drive the armed ones back to their valley!"

And with that, half of the flying people suddenly swooped down like a squadron of jet fighters and dove straight at the army. The gorilla guards, octopus guys, and potato bugs all screamed in terror at the wall of fire flying toward them and started running and rolling and galloping out of the square in a panic, stampeding through the streets toward the hills beyond the White House. The mole commander and the other members of the army who had formerly been citizens of Lesterville all took off running in the opposite direction, as if they simply wanted to get away from what seemed like a pretty unfriendly mob. Karen grabbed my hand and pulled me out of the square so we wouldn't get trampled by the running army guys. I looked back and saw Mr. Arthur just standing in the middle of it all, staring at his city for the last time.

"Chester!" Karen yelled back at him. "C'mon! Get out of there!"

But he didn't move. As we kept running, we saw him get swallowed up by the crowd of running guards who swarmed around him in their desperation to escape. Then we saw the flying people throw their torches down at all the buildings in Art's Square and beyond. The roar of a thousand torches flying through the air made it sound like a squadron of jet fighters was dive-bombing the city, and the streaks of red flame streaming down through the air looked like a shower of meteors from outer space. The torches hit the sides and tops of all the structures, breaking through windows and puncturing the thin walls.

**WHOOSH!** The buildings burst into flames immediately, going up like piles of oily rags. Whatever wood and other materials the city was made out of seemed like they were about the most flammable things that could have possibly been used. Within seconds, all of Art's Square was on fire and burning so brightly that it felt like the backs of our bodies were going to melt as we ran away. I looked up and saw Foo flying above us, keeping an eye on Karen and me as we ran through the street and past the theater where *Hamlet* was playing. As I looked back at the theater, it, too, exploded into flames, Mr. Arthur's picture on the marquee melting like the face of that Nazi guy in *Raiders of the Lost Ark*.

"Hey, Iggy," Karen said as we sprinted along. "Just for the record, even though things probably didn't turn out the way you imagined they would, well . . . I thought the way you handled yourself back there was really smart. Probably smarter than I would have done it. I guess you're not such an idiot after all."

I looked at her to make sure that she wasn't just making fun of me, but she actually seemed sincere. She smiled at me and it was a really nice moment right up until one of the skyscrapers behind us fell over and burning debris exploded all around us.

As we zigzagged through the fiery deluge, I looked ahead and saw that all the army guys were running past the White House and over the hill that led to the gold mines, as the cloud of flying people chased behind them, driving them back to the valley where they used to live.

Peepup and Feep Feep suddenly appeared through the crowd, dodging desperately to avoid being knocked over by the panicking guards. They ran over to us, Feep Feep holding Peepup's arm and dragging his slithering coils along.

"Herbert got away!" yelled Feep Feep. "As soon as he saw the fires start, he pushed us down and ran into the White House."

Karen looked at me. "If he has that machine you told us about, then he might be trying to escape."

"Fine," I said, confused why Karen would even care. "Let him go. He's a jerk."

"Iggy, you don't get it," she yelled as the roar of Lesterville on fire practically drowned out her voice. "If he escapes in that machine, then we may never have another chance to get out of here."

"Oh, man, you're right," I said, suddenly excited at the thought of getting to see my parents and friends again. "Let's go!"

As we took off sprinting toward the White House, I looked up at Foo, who was flying above us. She smiled down at me. Suddenly feeling weird, I forced a smile back at her. As much as I wanted to go home, I hated the idea of leaving this beautiful flying girl who liked me and believed in me. I would never have anything this great happen to me back in our frequency, I thought. There was no way.

Before I could even process that depressing realization, I saw a bunch of flying people who were chasing the army bank off and fly with their torches over the White House. My eyes went wide. If they set that place on fire with the transporter inside, Karen and I wouldn't be going anywhere.

Karen and I ran through the fence and then across the lawn to the front door as the flying people gathered overhead. They stopped when they saw Karen and me heading for the door and hovered over the White House, torches crackling. Then Herfta came flying over quickly and hovered in front of his people.

"Iggy and Karen, we
must also destroy this house,"
he called down to us. "It is the
will of the people."

"I don't know," I called up to Herfta.
"There seems to be an awful lot of burning
going on right now. And —"

Before I could tell them we needed to go inside to find the
machine, suddenly Herbert Golonski burst out of the front
door. He pushed Karen away violently, then grabbed me and
held what I immediately knew to be a gun against my head.

"Burn this building and I'll kill him," Herbert yelled up at
Herfta.

My eyes darted over to Karen, who was getting up slowly,
afraid to freak out Herbert. Herbert had the barrel of the gun
pressed so tightly against my temple, I thought it was going
to break through my skull and kill me without even firing.

The flying people all looked confused, clearly never having seen a gun before. Herbert saw this, then quickly took the gun away from my head and fired it into the ground at my feet. Dirt exploded everywhere as all the creatures around us jumped a mile. Herbert then quickly put the now hot gun barrel back against my head and yelled, "The next one goes into his brain."

"Release the boy," Herfta called down. "There is no escape from any of this."

"Fly away and leave this building intact," Herbert yelled back. "I have nothing to do with any of this. You have taken your revenge against Chester. Your revenge should not extend to me."

"We know who you are," said Herfta. "We have seen what you have done to the ground creatures in your camp. We know that you are taking the yellow rock from the ground. You are responsible for all that has happened here as much as is your president. Now, release the boy and get away from the building."

I could feel Herbert was breathing hard and I could only imagine his eyes darting around as he tried to figure out what to do. I saw Karen was ready to pounce on him but clearly there was no way she could do it without getting me killed. I looked up at Foo, who was hovering above, looking helpless.

"You have five seconds to leave," Herbert yelled up at the flying people, who stared down at him, not moving, their torches burning brightly. "Five."

"Let him go," Karen said calmly to Herbert. "Nothing's going to stop them."

"Four."

"Father, do what he says!" yelled Foo at her father.

"Three." Herbert's count was starting to sound angrier. He wasn't fooling around.

"*Please*, don't hurt him," Karen said, sounding like she actually cared about me.

"Two!"

My heart skipped a beat as I felt Herbert's arms tense around me and the gun push hard against my head. I heard everybody gasp as I prepared to find out just what it felt like to have my head blown off.

"ONE —"

"RAAAAARRRRR!!!" Suddenly, from out of nowhere, I saw a blur of something shoot past the corner of my eye. I heard Herbert scream and then the gun dropped from my temple as he was knocked sideways.

I looked and saw the cat who thought it was a dog hanging onto Herbert Golonski's face with its claws as it bit him over and over again, its back legs kicking furiously against his neck, scratching his skin. It really looked painful as Herbert rolled around shouting, "Get it off!" as he tried to pull the cat away from his head. Karen ran forward, kicked Herbert's gun away, and pulled me up as Foo flew in and hugged me.

"Stop!" I yelled at the cat. "Let him go."

The cat immediately jumped off Herbert and leaped up into my arms, licking my face like crazy. Herbert's face was bloody and he lay there dazed, trying to catch his breath, looking like he was in major pain. Then we heard the sound of many voices. We turned and saw a huge crowd of creatures from the city heading toward the White House. Many of them were carrying the torches that the flying people had thrown down onto Lesterville. And then, coming from the direction of the gold camps, we saw all the slaves and prisoners marching our way.

The crowd walked up and surrounded the White House. They looked like they wouldn't be happy until even this building had been destroyed. It was pretty scary, since the creatures had all seemed so harmless up until now. Apparently you can only push people so far.

Karen and I stared at them, unsure what they were going to do. Herbert sat up and saw what a bad situation he was in the middle of. Foo looked around at the crowd and then said to me, "They really didn't like Mr. Arthur, did they?"

And all of a sudden, the creatures lobbed a volley of torches through the air. The flaming projectiles crashed through the windows of the White House just as Mr. Arthur ran through the crowd. The house started on fire as he stopped and stared, looking almost resigned to the fact that he was losing everything he had made.

"Nooo!" yelled Herbert as he jumped up and ran into the house.

"There's no way he loves gold that much," Karen said, turning to me. "He must have that machine in there that can take us back. C'mon! Before it's too late."

I looked at Karen, then at the White House, which was quickly starting to burn more and more. The thought of running into a raging fire didn't seem at all like a good idea to me, and yet the thought of never being able to get home again didn't seem to be a great option, either.

I turned to Foo, then put the cat who thought it was a dog by her feet.

"I have to do this, Foo," I said as she stared into my eyes, confused. "Thank you for liking me." I then leaned in and kissed her cheek, very gently, so as not to hurt her. She smiled at me, then nodded understandingly. I bent down and rubbed the top of the cat's head, then said, "Thanks for saving me. Now you've got to take care of Foo." The cat licked my hand, then looked up and meowed at her.

"Iggy," said Karen. "We've gotta go."

I turned to Karen and said, "Yeah, I know."

And with that, we ran into the burning house.

# 36

## TIME TO GO

The house was quickly filling with thick black smoke. It burned our eyes and made it almost impossible to see.

"It's upstairs," I yelled to Karen over the sound of the roaring fire and all the glass breaking from the heat.

We ran up the stairs as flames leaped up the walls and spread out across the carpet. The bottom floor was burning so fast that I didn't know how much time we had to get to the secret room on the second level. And I hoped like crazy that the machine I had seen would actually take us back to our frequency. Maybe it was just some sort of weighing scale and Herbert *was* nuts and *was* simply running inside to get burned up with his gold. He seemed too smart to do that but when everything's falling apart, who knows what some people will do?

We got to the top of the stairs and ran toward the green door at the other end of the hallway. Smoke was starting to come up through the gaps in the floor. We could feel the heat of the fire through the bottoms of our shoes as we ran. It wouldn't be long before the downstairs ceiling burned completely and the second floor collapsed. "Oh, man," I said as the realization that we might be going back to our home frequency washed over me. "Dad's gonna kill me when he finds out I lost his Shakespeare book."

"Let's hope we get home alive so he *can* kill you!" Karen yelled over her shoulder.

We ran up to the green door and I pulled it open.

Herbert Golonski was frantically picking up the gold bars that were stacked against the wall outside of the machine and tossing them under its arch. He was sweating and cursing loudly to himself. Flames were starting to appear through the floor around the outer edge of the room. A big burst of fire suddenly flared up underneath the pile of gold he was taking bars off.

He screamed as the flames made him jump back, then shook his hands in pain. He looked up and saw us standing in the doorway.

"You haven't stopped anything!" he yelled at us as the

fire started to melt the gold bars against the wall. "No one can stop the inevitable!"

He looked at the bars that weren't in the machine as they began to sweat and then dissolve into small rivers of yellow metal, dripping down the pile like butterscotch on an ice-cream sundae. He looked upset, the way you do when you realize that something you've been working on for a long time is now all about to be for nothing. He then said, "I can't believe I have to come back here again," and ran to the machine. He quickly ran his fingers in some weird pattern over the computer screen and stood underneath the arch.

"See you back home!" he said with a strange smile.

Everything under the arch began to glow as a loud, low humming started to drown out the sound of the fire. As smoke came up through the floorboards, the whole room began to shake. Suddenly, Mr. Arthur pushed past us and ran into the room as he clutched my dad's Shakespeare book in his hand.

"Wait for me!" he yelled, and dove at the arch, which was glowing so brightly we could barely look at it.

***BOOM!*** There was a huge explosion that knocked Karen and me off our feet as a bright flash of light hit our faces like a burst of hot air. We fell back onto the floor, which was now very hot from the fire downstairs, and then both of us sat up quickly to see what had happened.

Under the machine's arch, there was nothing.

Herbert Golonski, Mr. Arthur, Dad's book, and the bars of gold were gone.

As Karen and I exchanged a look, flames exploded up through the floor behind us.

"Get in the machine! Quick!" she yelled as we jumped up and ran over to it.

The smoke was now very thick and pools of liquid gold were running onto the floor in flowing puddles. We got to the machine and looked at the screen that Herbert had waved his hand over.

"I think I saw what he did," I said to Karen right before I went into a coughing fit from the smoke.

"Then do it!" she yelled. "Two more coughs and we'll be out of time."

I waved my hand over the screen and moved my first and second fingers back and forth quickly, a move that I had seen Herbert do.

Suddenly, the arch started to glow again. We stood underneath it as the rumbling once more grew loud. Flames burst up through the floorboards as the green door started on fire and the hallway outside the door collapsed.

"Hurry up, machine!" Karen yelled as the rumbling became deafening and the room started to shake. The wall next to the melting pile of leftover gold caved in and flames shot out of the next room, burning the hairs on my right arm.

We squinted and held our hands over our ears and fell against each other as the sound and light and shaking became unbearable. And just when I thought I was going to pass out . . .

**BOOM!**

There was a blinding flash of light and I suddenly felt like all the air around my body exploded inward. I fell onto the ground and felt Karen fall down next to me.

And then suddenly everything was quiet.

\*     \*     \*

I felt dirt under my hands. My eyes were temporarily blind from the burst of light, sort of like after somebody takes your picture with a flash camera. I was breathing heavily as I tried to get the oxygen into my lungs and the smoke out of them. The air around us was no longer hot from the fire, and a warm, wet breeze blew over my face.

Slowly, I sat up as I heard Karen stirring next to me. I looked over and as my eyes began to adjust, I saw that she was also sitting up.

"Are you okay?" I asked.

"Yeah," she said, sounding a bit disoriented. "Are you?"

"I think so."

"Are we home?" she said as she rubbed her eyes to have a look at the frequency she had been away from for so long.

But that wasn't what we saw.

Because we were someplace completely different, a place that was way weirder than the frequency we had just left.

I didn't know where the heck we were, but we sure weren't home.

And we were now, whether we wanted to be or not, officially Frequenauts.